Tangled

Also from Rebecca Zanetti

SCORPIUS SYNDROME SERIES
Scorpius Rising
Mercury Striking
Shadow Falling
Justice Ascending
Storm Gathering (September 19, 2017)

DARK PROTECTORS
Fated
Claimed
Tempted
Hunted
Consumed
Provoked
Twisted
Shadowed
Tamed
Marked
Teased
Tricked
Tangled
Talen (June 6, 2017)

REALM ENFORCERS
Wicked Ride
Wicked Edge
Wicked Burn
Wicked Kiss (July 4, 2017)
Wicked Bite (August 1, 2017)

SIN BROTHERS
Forgotten Sins
Sweet Revenge

Blind Faith
Total Surrender

BLOOD BROTHERS
Deadly Silence
Lethal Lies
Twisted Truths

MAVERICK MONTANA
Against the Wall
Under the Covers
Rising Assets
Over the Top

Tangled

A Dark Protectors—Reese Family
Novella

By Rebecca Zanetti

1001 Dark Nights

EVIL EYE
CONCEPTS

Tangled
A Dark Protectors—Reese Family Novella
By Rebecca Zanetti

Copyright 2017 Rebecca Zanetti
ISBN: 978-1-945920-14-1

Foreword: Copyright 2014 M. J. Rose

Published by Evil Eye Concepts, Incorporated

Acknowledgments from the Author

The 1001DN project started as an exciting marketing plan for authors that has turned into so very much more. All of the people involved, from the creators to the consultants to the authors are truly amazing, and I'm honored to be included.

For many of us, this group has turned into a soft place to land in a wild industry.

We've become friends and confidants, and it's difficult to describe how much that means to me.

Elizabeth Berry, you've taken a love of reading and a brilliant marketing mind and created something really special. Thank you for including me in your world. I hope you never need to bury a body, but if you do, I'm there for you.

MJ Rose, you're a marketing genius with a truly creative mind, and you've done a marvelous job along with Liz. I don't think you'd need help burying a body, but if you ever need a buddy for a lengthy shopping trip, I'm your gal.

Jillian Stein, you've saved whatever sanity I might have retained throughout the years. I trust you with everything, and I can't thank you enough for all that you do. If we had to bury a body, I have no doubt you'd color-code and calendar the plan with a cool trailer to go with it. It'd be a well-organized adventure for us that would end with a Twilight marathon.

Steve Berry, thank you for your generosity with sharing your insights and experience in the book industry. Thank you also for your tremendous sense of humor in dealing with, well, all of us. I know I'm a peach, but that Lexi Blake is a loveable scamp.

Thank you to Kimberly Guidroz, Pam Jamison, Fedora Chen, and Kasi Alexander for their dedication and awesome insights.

Thanks also to Asha Hossain, who creates absolutely fantastic book covers.

As always, a lot of love and a huge thank you goes to Big Tone, Gabe and Karly, my amazing family who is so supportive.

Finally, thank you to Rebecca's Rebels, my street team, who have been so generous with their time and friendship. Thank you to Minga Portillo for her excellent leadership of the team. And last, but not least, thank you to all of my readers who spend time with my characters.

The Dark Protectors are coming back with new stories in 2018, and I hope you like them!

~ RAZ

Sign up for the 1001 Dark Nights Newsletter
and be entered to win a Tiffany Key necklace.

There's a contest every month!

Go to www.1001DarkNights.com to subscribe.

As a bonus, all subscribers will receive a free
1001 Dark Nights story
The First Night
by Lexi Blake & M.J. Rose

One Thousand and One Dark Nights

Once upon a time, in the future...

*I was a student fascinated with stories and learning.
I studied philosophy, poetry, history, the occult, and
the art and science of love and magic. I had a vast
library at my father's home and collected thousands
of volumes of fantastic tales.*

*I learned all about ancient races and bygone
times. About myths and legends and dreams of all
people through the millennium. And the more I read
the stronger my imagination grew until I discovered
that I was able to travel into the stories... to actually
become part of them.*

*I wish I could say that I listened to my teacher
and respected my gift, as I ought to have. If I had, I
would not be telling you this tale now.
But I was foolhardy and confused, showing off
with bravery.*

*One afternoon, curious about the myth of the
Arabian Nights, I traveled back to ancient Persia to
see for myself if it was true that every day Shahryar
(Persian: شهريار, "king") married a new virgin, and then
sent yesterday's wife to be beheaded. It was written
and I had read, that by the time he met Scheherazade,
the vizier's daughter, he'd killed one thousand
women.*

Something went wrong with my efforts. I arrived in the midst of the story and somehow exchanged places with Scheherazade – a phenomena that had never occurred before and that still to this day, I cannot explain.

Now I am trapped in that ancient past. I have taken on Scheherazade's life and the only way I can protect myself and stay alive is to do what she did to protect herself and stay alive.

Every night the King calls for me and listens as I spin tales. And when the evening ends and dawn breaks, I stop at a point that leaves him breathless and yearning for more. And so the King spares my life for one more day, so that he might hear the rest of my dark tale.

As soon as I finish a story... I begin a new one... like the one that you, dear reader, have before you now.

Chapter 1

Two weeks on the hunt, and now Theo Reese was dressed like a wanker from one of those popular spy movies. He tugged on the black bow tie and fully committed himself to killing the woman who'd forced him to wear a tuxedo. After chasing her through New York, London, Edinburgh, and now back to New York, he was more than ready to grip her slim neck in both his hands.

Then he'd squeeze until her stunning blue eyes bugged.

Maybe. Okay. He wouldn't kill her. Even as pissed as he was, he'd never harm a woman. Well, probably. This one had taken subterfuge to a whole new level, so he would like to scare her a little. Plus, the woman was a witch, so it wasn't like she couldn't defend herself. Creating fire out of air was like breathing for her people.

Chatter and the clinking of glasses filled the opulent ballroom of New York's most exclusive hotel. Women in long sparkling dresses and men in tuxedos milled around, drinking champagne and laughing. Christmas lights blinked green and red from trees placed in every corner.

Discreet waiters refilled glasses and offered canapés.

Theo sighed. He wanted a steak, damn it. Little mushrooms filled with green stuff would just make him hungrier.

Where the hell was she?

His contacts had said she'd be attending the fundraiser to save some otter in some forest somewhere, and he'd had to pretty much give up a kidney to get a ticket. A gold-encrusted ticket. He didn't get it. Why not just save the money on tickets, clothes, food, and drink…and give it to the damn otters? Buy them all a new river and forest somewhere.

He caught a scent. Through the heavy perfumes and fragrant appetizers, a scent he knew well beckoned him. Woman, intrigue, and Irish bluebells from her native home.

Lifting his head, he followed his nose. Even for a vampire, he had enhanced senses.

Her laugh, tinkling and surprisingly deep, had him turning left.

Ah. There she was. He'd finally found the witch. His entire body tightened, and the blood rushed from his head right to his cock. From one little sighting of her. Fuck. Taking several deep breaths, he calmed his body and cleared his mind.

Ginny O'Toole wore a sapphire colored gown that matched her eyes perfectly. The bodice was old fashioned, glimmering with sparkles, and narrowed to an impossibly small waist. Her breasts were full, her hair naturally white-blonde, her skin flawless, and her stature petite. Three hundred years ago, she'd been too thin for popularity. Fifty years ago, she'd been the ideal woman. Now, in the day and age of curves and diversity, she stood out as almost unreal. As more of a doll than a real woman.

An air of fragility clung to her, in direct opposition to strong and fierce modern woman.

Yet men flocked to her, quick to give protection, just as much today as in the past. The morons didn't realize that her pretty face masked a predator. One who used wiles and weakness to get what she wanted. False weakness. Oh, physically she lacked strength. But mentally, she was a manipulative bitch.

She was talking to a tall man who had his back to Theo. Short blond hair, wide shoulders, strong energy. Was that a shifter? Yeah. Feline. Probably lion.

Theo launched into motion, easily winding through the human throng, and reached them in seconds.

Ginny's eyes widened and then her mask dropped back into place. "Theo." She smiled, and if he couldn't hear her hammering heartbeat, he would've been fooled into believing she was actually pleased to see him. Since she'd been running from him for weeks after hacking into the main computer at one of his family's estates, he knew that to be a lie. "Theo Reese, please meet Jack Jacobson," she said.

Jacobson turned and held out a hand. "It's a pleasure."

Theo shook his hand, lowering his chin. The shifter shaking his hand was an information broker by the name of Jackson McIntosh. They'd never done business, but Theo had seen dossiers on the guy. "Jack Jacobson?" he murmured, barely flashing his canines. "That's a nice pseudonym."

Jack nodded. "I like it."

"Your business here is concluded," Theo said, releasing Jacobson and grasping Ginny by the elbow. Her bones felt fragile beneath his hand, so he loosened his hold automatically.

She didn't struggle, as if she could. Instead, her smile widened. "Actually, it is. Please get back to me with your answer soon, Jack."

Heat rushed down Theo's back. The woman thought he was so daft he wouldn't figure out what she was trying to sell? He had an idea of what information she was looking to get rid of, and that ended right now. "There's a chance your deal might be dead in the water," he said evenly.

Jack's green eyes twinkled. "Perhaps." Then he sobered, his gaze moving to Theo's hand. "Let her go."

Jesus. The woman brought out the defender in everybody. Even criminal middlemen who were well known to broker anything—legal or illegal. "No," Theo returned.

"You are so very sweet to worry about me." Ginny patted Jack's arm with her free hand. "Theo and I are old friends. No need for concern."

Old friends, his ass. Theo didn't bother to smile. If she wanted to play the polite game, she could damn well do it by herself. He didn't play games. Ever.

Jack's eyes narrowed. "You certain?"

"I am," Ginny said softly. "Theo and I have some business to conduct as well. It was lovely to see you, Jack."

Theo might just throw up. "Bye, Jack."

The shifter nodded, gave him one hard look, and turned on his polished loafers. Seconds later, he'd disappeared into the throng.

Ginny sighed. "Kindly remove your hand."

"Not a chance in hell," Theo returned, drawing her nearer. "And I'm warning you. You try to create a scene, you cause any problem, and I'll not care about collateral damage for once. You're coming with me, and we're retrieving the Benjamin file. Right now."

Her eyes widened fully, and she planted a small hand against her bare upper chest. "The Benjamin file? What in the world is that?"

He barked out a laugh. Truly, he couldn't help it. "Ginny, from day one, your act hasn't worked on me, and you know it." That was why she'd chosen his older brother to manipulate and use a century ago. Jared had fallen for her helpless act, thought he was in love, and had had his heart broken when she'd mated another male instead of him. Well, he'd thought it had been broken. Now that he'd found his true mate, he knew the difference. "So knock it off," Theo finished.

"Theo," Ginny whispered. "I truly do not know anything about a Benjamin file. What in the world is that?"

It was the computer file that detailed all of Theo's family's holdings and dealings...even the illegal ones. It could bring down and bankrupt his entire family, and most importantly, his Uncle Benjamin. Benny was a crazy thousand-year-old vampire who would easily cut off Theo's head for losing the file. "I don't have time for games. Where's the flash drive?" he asked quietly.

She shrugged creamy shoulders. "You know I don't understand computers."

The woman could lie. Well. But Theo knew better. "You firebombed our entire system, and now that flash drive is the only record we have. It proves ownership of everything we have." It also held files they'd used to blackmail others during the years, which was an acceptable way of doing business in the immortal world. He leaned down until his nose nearly touched hers. "I'm losing patience."

Pink bloomed across her high cheekbones. "Really, Theo. Ownership records are easy to find these days. Obtain the title deeds in every place you own property. Stocks and businesses have records."

He breathed out, his lungs heating. Many records had no paper trail, and she knew it. The blackmail info, and the family history, were both hidden on purpose. And even so, he didn't have time to traverse the world looking for what legitimate documentation he could find. "Where's the data?" Hopefully she'd been too busy running from him and trying to sell the files that she hadn't had time to really go through them.

He had to get the Green Rock file before anybody else read it. The damn thing might result in his entire family being killed by their current allies. It'd also break his brother Chalton's heart if he learned the truth. The Realm, his adopted family, would turn on him. "Tell me, Ginny. Now."

The witch sighed. "I'm getting a headache. Would you please just stop stalking me?"

He barely kept from glaring at her. This close, he could see dark circles beneath her eyes. Beneath his hand, her arm trembled. Running from him had taken a toll on her. He tried to steel his heart against that fact, because she'd use it against him. "Let's go to my hotel and have a nice meal." Maybe if he got some food into her, the color would return to her pretty face. "We can talk about the file there."

"No." Her pink lips turned down in a pout.

"Does that look actually work on people?" he asked, truly curious.

Fire flashed in her intriguing eyes.

Ah, he'd gotten to her. "I guess it does." He faulted his gender for being easy marks. Not once had he ever understood why she played at being so helpless. Why not be straight up? Hell, if he didn't need to get that file back, *he'd* probably be an easy mark for her if she was honest with him for two whole seconds. "You don't need games with beauty like yours, Ginny."

Surprise, the genuine kind, tilted her lips. "I thought you hated the way I look."

Right. Vampires always hated beauty. "No. I dislike the way you pretend to be something you're not. The way you look is...good." Unbelievably stunning, to be honest. But he couldn't give her an inch, or he'd be letting his entire family down. And probably signing their death sentence. "So drop the act, would you?"

She shook her head as if she was in on a joke he couldn't

fathom. Regret darkened those blue eyes for just a second, enhancing the tired circles beneath them. "You only see what you want to see, Theo."

What the hell did that mean? He leaned in. "Explain."

Her slim shoulders went back. "I can't. But you're right. We do need to talk. Let's go discuss this somewhere else."

Good. She was finally going to work with him. He looked toward the nearest exit. "I agree. Let's get out of here. Why are you caring about otters, anyway?"

She blinked. "Otters?"

He gestured around.

She laughed, the sound spontaneous and so sexy it hurt. "Oh, Theo. This is a fundraiser for Other Tracks. An international nonprofit that fights the sex trafficking of children across the globe? I donate every year."

He straightened. Was she lying? "Oh." That did seem a lot more important than otters. He studied her, fighting the urge to believe her. She was so damn good at tricking men. Right now, he had other worries. "Let's go."

She sighed, her shoulders hunching. "Very well." Pivoting, she stumbled into him.

Pain flared through his arm. Heat rushed through his veins, and his head grew heavy. Gravity claimed him, and he started to fall.

"Sorry," she whispered, helping him down to the floor and setting his back to the wall.

He blinked, his tongue thickening as he saw the small syringe in her hand. The last thought he had before passing completely out was to wonder where such a curve-hugging dress had pockets.

Then he was out.

Chapter 2

Ginny rushed into the suite in her ancient hotel, running for the bedroom to quickly pack. She'd been waylaid too many times on her way out of the ball, but she'd had appearances to keep up. This identity was one she cherished, and she'd fight to keep it. She considered it her good one. The one that did honorable things like help organizations like Other Tracks.

Oh, Theo would only be out for a short time. The sedative she'd brought had been created for shifters, just in case Jack had tried something. It would take a vampire like Theo down, but not for long.

She threw clothing into her suitcase, trying to keep her energy up. After working the ball for two hours, she was spent and needed rest. Grabbing her sparkly flats, she quickly exchanged them for her three-inch heels, packing those in the bag. Where the heck should she run? She had to stay close in case Jack was able to broker a deal. Her final deal. Then she was out.

The hotel was in the seedier side of town, so no way would Theo look for her there.

Theo Reese couldn't be allowed to screw this up for her.

Damn that vampire. He was far too smart and sexy for her peace of mind. Not once, *not once*, had he ever fallen for the character she most often played in life. While that intrigued her, totally against her will, she didn't have time to explore it. Not now. Not when she was so close.

She grabbed her suitcase and the laptop bag, running into the living area.

The door crashed open and banged against the wall. Twice.

She halted, her lungs seizing.

Theo Reese stood in the doorway, his tux askew, fury across his hard face. All vampires had hard faces. Yet Theo's was a rock-like formation chiseled into rugged planes and fierce angles that had haunted her dreams more than once through the years. His body was muscled and tight, yet he moved with the grace of a panther shifter. Deadly and sure. His thick brown hair was several shades lighter than his midnight black eyes, which right now swirled with an anger that stole her breath.

She swallowed, looking for an escape.

"In that dress, you'll never make it down the fire escape." He stepped inside and shut the door behind himself. Well, he shut what was left of the door. "Your sedative didn't last long."

The bastard probably had the metabolism of a demon. Damn vampire. "I said I was sorry." She dropped her bags and let her voice go breathy. "But...but I had no choice, Theo." Yes. Good tremble on the last.

"Bullshit." He crossed his arms over his broad chest, staring down from at least an additional foot of height.

She coughed. Nobody swore at her. Ever.

He lowered his chin. "I swear, Ginny. If you don't drop the fucking act, I'm going to lose my temper. You don't want that."

No. She truly did not want that. Why hadn't she taken time to change out of the ball gown? It was nearly impossible to fight in the darn thing. No wonder it had taken so long for women to reach equality in this new world. Their very clothing had held them back. "Theo, there's no need to get nasty," she said, her mind spinning for a plan.

"You haven't seen nasty. Yet." He cocked his head to the side and focused on her laptop bag. "Is my flash drive in there?"

"No," she said honestly. "I have no idea what flash drive you're talking about." Aye, she lied that time.

His focus slashed back to her face. "Ah, baby. That's the first time we've had this type of conversation. I have a baseline for you now. You have a tell when you lie."

"I do not," she burst out before she could stop herself.

His smile was slow and somehow dangerous. "You do."

"I'm a natural redhead," she spat, forgetting all about how tired she was.

"Lie."

She breathed out. "I once climbed Mt. Rainier."

He blinked. "Truth."

Damn it. "I was very much in love with your brother."

Red flared across Theo's face, and he took a minute before responding this time. "Lie," he said thoughtfully.

"I love garlic," she said, her heart speeding up.

"Lie," he said instantly.

God. How was he doing that? "I am nearly addicted to Irish whiskey," she said quietly.

He glanced down her dress. "Truth, but that's hard to believe."

Was he guessing? So far, he'd been correct every time. "I want to sleep with you," she whispered.

He grinned, making him look almost boyish. "Truth."

Her breath relaxed. "Wrong."

"No." He moved toward her. "Feel free to lie to yourself, lady. But that was the truth."

She couldn't help but take a step back. Sure, she'd thought about him. More than she should have. But she did not want to have sex with the damn vampire. "You're such a bastard."

"True sentiment but a lie overall. My parents were married and mated," he returned, continuing slowly toward her as if he had all the time in the world.

She stumbled back and held up a hand. "Stop."

"Why?" he asked, not stopping.

"You're scaring me, Theo," she said, trying for simpering.

He stopped cold. "The wimpy tone is bullshit, but I *am* scaring you." His lip quirked as if he wasn't quite sure what to do with that information. "If scaring you gets me what I want, then I'll do it. I'm prepared to do almost anything, Ginny. Don't make me."

Now he was telling the full truth. Just how far would he go to get back the Benjamin file? For the first time, she actually doubted her ability to get a job done. "I really don't know what flash drive you're talking about." She kept her voice level this time and looked him right in the eye.

"Lie," he whispered, slowly shaking his head but somehow managing to keep eye contact. "Oh, you're good. But that was a lie."

She breathed in and settled her stance beneath the long gown without giving her intent away. "Why don't we call Jared?" Maybe big brother could talk some sense into Theo.

"He's on his honeymoon," Theo said.

She tried to drum up some sense of hurt, but truth be told, she was happy for the vampire. Jared was a good guy, and he deserved happiness. The vamp in front of her was not a good guy, and he had a hell of an ego. Anger pushed through her fear. "I'm not dealing with Reese junior here." If she could get him angry enough, maybe he'd make a mistake. "Send in the older boys, would you?"

Theo's smile was predatory, plain and simple. "Sorry. My brothers are busy. You'll have to deal with me."

His dark tone licked right across her skin. For years, she'd tried to avoid Theo Reese. He was too smart, too strong...too male. The born soldier in the family. Her damsel act had never worked on him, and that was damn unfortunate. Men were usually idiots, which suited her purposes just fine. Normally. This male...did not suit. "You're unreasonable, and you won't listen," she said softly, breathing in to push out her breasts over the top of the bustier.

His eyes flared, and satisfaction heated through her. Her breath sped up along with her heart rate. When was the last time a man had provided a challenge for her? He might read lies, but she read people, and this male wanted her. She could use that. As much as she might not want to do so, she had a job to do. A critical one. This time, she stepped toward him. "Listen to me, Theo."

His head lifted, while a veil drew down over his eyes. "I'm listening." His voice lowered to a hoarse growl.

Her abdomen heated, and her breasts grew heavy. "I—"

He wrapped a warm hand around her neck, stopping her words.

She stilled. How had he moved so quickly? Her gaze snapped up to meet his.

"No more lying," he said softly. Way too softly.

A tremble shook her that had nothing to do with fear. Her

nerves flashed to fully alive, and her skin sensitized. What the hell was happening to her? Her clothes were suddenly too restrictive. She licked her lips.

His gaze tracked her tongue. Tension exploded around them, rolling through the room.

She wanted to retreat a step, but her legs wouldn't cooperate. "Theo—"

Pressing his thumb and forefinger beneath where her jaw met her neck, he drew her toward him. "You don't speak unless it's the truth. Got it?"

Fury speared through her. "Think you can stop me?" She lost any hint of helplessness.

"Yes." His gaze dropped to her mouth. "Try me."

God. Was he saying what she thought he was saying? Her mind fuzzed. No. This couldn't happen. She knew. She *just knew* that being kissed by Theo Reese would change her world. Considering her world was full of intrigue, pain, and lies right now...that might not be so bad. But getting involved with him would be a disaster. Especially right now. "Release me because this is a very bad idea," she whispered.

A muscle ticked in his jaw. "That wasn't a lie."

"No." It wasn't.

"Where's the Benjamin file?" His gaze traveled up from her lips to her eyes.

All Saints, she could get lost in those midnight black eyes. This close, she could see different shades. Were there different shades of black? She hadn't thought so before. Now, she could see them. Ah. Vampire eyes. Wait a minute. The vamps had tertiary eye colors that came out in times of stress or great emotion or supposedly during sex. Jared's were just a darker black, which she'd seen once when he'd been in a fight as a kid. Chalton, the middle brother, had a deep blue that was almost black and didn't look much different from his normal color. She only knew that because of a background file she'd read on him. There was no such background file on Theo. Unfortunately.

Theo leaned closer. "Ginny?"

"What other color are your eyes?" she blurted.

He blinked. Once and then twice. "The only way you'll ever know that is if you're naked."

Naked. He said *naked*. She gulped down a swallow. Images of Theo sans clothing, over her, slid through her mind, down her body, and landed hard between her legs. Was it possible to faint from desire? Oh, she was a master at pretending to faint. But now, her knees actually wobbled. "How improper," she said, fighting her hardest to keep her voice mild.

"The last thing in the world you need is proper." His voice was even milder.

He wanted to play? Fine. She could play. "What do I need, Theo?" she asked in her flirtiest voice, trying to toss her head at the same time. His firm hand made it difficult, but she gave it a good effort, sending her thick hair tumbling down her back.

A growl rumbled up his chest and heated the air between them. "Not something you'd enjoy," he said, his hold tightening just enough to give warning. "Why the hell aren't you burning me? Are you that desperate to appear weak?"

The words slapped her in the face. Only training kept her from reacting. "You're not worth the effort."

His head tilted just slightly, in a curiously dangerous way. "That hurt you. What I said. Why?"

Was he a damn mind reader? Bollocks. Witches used quantum physics, among other sciences, to create plasma fire out of the air around them. It was an excellent weapon, and if she had the ability to use it, she would've already burned off every hair on his head. "You didn't hurt me."

"Lie." He said the last softly—thoughtfully. His brows drew down. "I'm not releasing you until you give me an answer."

"To which question?" she snapped.

He drew her even closer. "Both. Where's my file, and why can't you create fire?"

"I don't have your file, and I can create fire," she said.

He breathed out. "Kind of true and kind of false. Interesting. So you don't have the file right now, which makes sense. A smart thief would've hidden it elsewhere. And you can create fire, but you're unable to do so right now. Why is that?"

"You're crazy."

"Maybe. But we're not moving until you give me the truth."

She had no choice. Shoving both arms up, she broke his hold, and then just as quickly punched him in the eye.

He reared back, grabbing his eye and snarling.

Lifting her skirts, she jumped and kicked him beneath the jaw. He flew back and hit the sofa.

She turned to run just as the front door blew open again, this time with fire. Heat flashed toward her and she screamed, ducking to avoid being burned.

Flames flashed right over her head.

Chapter 3

Theo reacted instantly, shoving off the sofa and covering Ginny with his body. He rolled them until she was behind the sofa, and then he jumped up to lunge for the door.

Plasma sailed into his chest. He ignored the pain, tackling two males into the hallway. Witches. Damn fucking fire-throwing witches. Both dressed in combat gear, already hurtling fire at him. He punched one guy right under the jaw, shattering it into pieces he could feel with his knuckles. The male went limp, knocked out. Theo back-flipped onto his feet, bounced once, and kicked the other guy in the temple.

The guy went down and just as quickly leaped up, head into Theo's gut. The force threw them both into the wall, denting the hard wood.

Two more men ran by them and into the dingy room.

Damn it. Ginny wasn't covered. Theo slammed his elbows down on his attacker's shoulders, dropping the guy to the ground. Then he punched with an uppercut, and the witch fell back onto his shoulders. Blue flames poured down his arms. He threw fire.

Shit.

Theo jumped to the side. The plasma ball hit the wall with a loud thud, and flames licked up the wood. Fire burned his arm, but he skidded on his knees, already punching for the witch's face. Blood arced, but he kept punching, ignoring the return hits, until the guy finally stopped moving.

"Asshole." Theo shoved to his feet and turned for the crappy room. The fire was spreading, and smoke filled the hallway. The alarms started blaring, and the sprinkler system ignited. Water streamed down, making the flames hiss. The smoke clogged his way. He shoved through it to see Ginny struggling between two men as they dragged her toward the door.

"Throw some fire, woman," Theo roared, pissed beyond belief.

The three paused, mouths agape. It would've been comical if he hadn't been so furious.

Ginny yanked free of one male and pivoted to punch the other in the eye. The guy reared back and slapped her across the face. Hard. The sound echoed even through the fire, alarm, and spraying water. Her head flew to the side with water matting her hair.

Theo lost his fucking mind.

With a roar that would've done a demon proud, he lunged for the guy, grabbing him around the neck and lifting. Fury and adrenaline giving him strength, Theo swung around and threw the bastard toward the wide window. The witch hit dead center and crashed through. He shrieked as he began pummeling toward the ground eight floors below.

Ginny turned toward Theo, her eyes wide with shock. "Oh my God. That was thick glass."

The other witch moved fast and grabbed her, yanking her against his chest with his arm banded around her throat. She clawed at his forearm, her eyes filling with tears.

"Let her go." Theo advanced through the smoke and spraying water toward the two.

"No." The witch tried to pull her toward the door. "I have a job to do."

"Why her?" Theo took another step, brushing soot out of his eyes.

The guy kept moving. "Don't know. Don't care."

So the men were just hired guns. It figured Ginny had more than one enemy out there, considering she was a thief. Theo couldn't have been her first mark. "I've already killed your buddy and knocked out the other two."

"Wasn't my buddy, and he's probably not dead," the guy returned, his eyes wild.

True. The witch had certainly hit the ground by now. He might not be dead, but he wouldn't be attempting any kidnappings for quite some time. Theo jerked his head toward Ginny, noting how pale she'd become. "What's she worth, anyway?"

"Twenty-five million." The guy studied him. "Considering you've taken out my team, want to split it?" Soot and water mangled through the guy's long blond hair, but his dark eyes were clear. Smart and calculating.

Ginny struggled against him, making little choking noises.

Theo paused and concentrated on her. "You can't create fire." She should've burned the shit out of the guy by now. Wait a minute. He focused back on the blond guy. "Did you know that? That she couldn't create fire?"

"No. I figured if she started to burn me, I'd just choke her out," the guy said congenially, as if chatting with a friend. "So. Do we have a deal or not?"

Theo paused, as if considering.

Ginny gasped. "Seriously? You're honestly thinking of making a deal?" Her voice came out a little squeaky. Soot marred her forehead, and a bruise was already forming on her left cheekbone where the asshole had hit her. "Theo?"

"Where's the file you stole from me?" he asked, stopping three feet away from the duo.

Her eyes bugged. "Are you jesting?"

He lifted a shoulder.

Sirens sounded in the distance.

The guy blanched. "Hey, we have to get out of here. Fast."

Theo nodded. "Seriously, Ginny. Can't you fight at all?"

"I hit you in the eye," she said, a little color filling her face. "It's been a long day." Her lips trembled, and she renewed her struggles, pushing back and obviously trying to toss the guy over her head. It wasn't even close as a contest. Strength-wise, she appeared tapped.

"What's wrong with you?" Theo murmured. Even though the guy was much larger, she was a witch and should at least have some moves. But she appeared as helpless as a human female. Would she really push her charade of helplessness in a situation like this? His gut churned. Either she was that dishonest…or there was something wrong with her. "Fight him."

"I'm trying." Tears filled her eyes, and damn if they didn't look real.

Men's shouts echoed up from the stairwell.

"They're coming. We have to go and meet my secondary team on floor two." The guy started dragging her toward the door. "I have two more men waiting for us, and they'll head this way if we don't hurry. Let's get out of here."

Theo nodded. "Okay. I'll take point." He ignored Ginny's gasp and started for the door, turning at the last second and punching the guy in the temple.

The guy fell back, and Theo followed him, nailing him directly in the throat.

Ginny sagged against the wall.

Theo grabbed her hand and her suitcase. "I hope you're as good in that dress as you act. We're taking the fire escape." All but dragging her, he hustled through the disaster of the hotel room for the far windows.

She grasped her laptop bag on the way, stumbling next to him. One of her sparkly shoes fell off, and she kept going, kicking off the other one. They looked slippery, so it was probably a good call. "We're eight floors up," she gasped through the smoke and streaming water.

"I know," he said grimly. "You can explain what the fuck is going on with you on the way down." If the humans or the other witches didn't catch them first.

* * * *

Ginny gathered her skirts the best she could and followed Theo down the hard metal fire escape. Snow and ice covered the metal, and a cold December wind blew hard against them. He'd gone first, no doubt preparing to catch her if she fell. The man had no clue how close she was to actually fainting. *Really* fainting. Her ears rang, and her entire body ached from her attempts to fight.

Tears gathered in her eyes from the damn unfairness of it all, and she angrily batted them away.

"Hurry, honey," Theo said from below her, gracefully going backward down the zillion steps.

Honey. He'd called her honey. And he'd kicked some serious witch butt when defending her. The idea warmed her entire chest, and she tried to ignore the feeling. They were enemies, and she had to remember that fact. If he won, she lost. So she'd have to figure a way out of this mess.

Once they were on the ground.

She swallowed and looked straight ahead at the worn brick. Staying at old and seedy hotels had advantages...mainly outdoor fire escapes. Her foot missed a rung, and she slipped. "Theo," she gasped, just as she fell.

He caught her around the waist on a landing. "Damn it." Grabbing her skirt, he ripped it across the bottom, leaving her legs bare from the knees down. "There. That should—" He paused and looked down at her ankle. "What the hell?"

"No time." She grabbed a rung and started heading down, ignoring the diamond and gold spiked ankle bracelet. The sirens sounded closer, and blue and red swirling lights cut through the darkness of the night. A firetruck rolled by the main street, and shouting voices echoed from up above.

Adrenaline gave her strength, and without the skirt hampering her, she quickly made it to the litter-covered street.

Theo jumped next to her and swung her up in his arms, turning and hurrying away from the emergency vehicles. Somehow he kept hold of her suitcase.

She jostled against his chest, clutching her laptop bag. "What are you doing?"

"Your feet are bare. There's glass and who knows what else on the ground." He wasn't even breathing heavily.

She tried to remain stiff in his arms, but her body relaxed right into his warmth. Theo was all muscled male strength around her, and for the first time in far too long, she felt safe. For the moment. Wrapping her arm around his neck to help him keep his balance, she gave in to temptation and rested her face against his neck.

They were both soaking wet and covered in soot, but somehow, he smelled good. Wild and masculine, with a hint of something spicy. His heart beat steadily against her chest, and she shut her eyes. Just for the second. Pretending that she was safe and belonged with him. For years, she'd fought her own battles, even while pretending to be helpless. While she was more than capable of taking care of herself, under normal circumstances, she had no problem being saved by somebody who cared for her.

It was too late to save her.

More importantly, Theo Reese didn't care for her. He saw her as the manipulative bitch who'd broken his brother's heart, and as a thief who could harm his family. "I didn't really hurt Jared, you know," she said softly, her lips moving against his warm skin.

Theo stiffened but kept moving through darkened alleys. "Yes, you did."

Her stomach ached. "He didn't love me. Not really. He loved the idea of how strong I made him feel back a million years ago."

"Maybe," Theo allowed.

She sighed. "If he'd really loved me, no way would he have let me mate somebody else. You know that." In fact, Jared had used his hurt ego to become a pirate on the open seas, which he'd truly loved. "Right?"

"There's truth to that," Theo said, his mouth next to her temple. "He's happy now, and that's all that matters. He found the right mate for him, without question."

"So stop being mad at me." She hated how needy she sounded, but fighting just took too much out of her. "Please."

"Give me the file back and we'll talk about it," he said, making another turn in the dark night. The sirens and sounds of the crowd slowly disappeared. Snow started falling, mixing with the soot covering them both.

"Where are we going?" she asked, her body beginning to shut down.

He slipped on the ice and quickly regained his footing, not slowing in the slightest. "I have a car around the next block."

She couldn't get into a vehicle with him, but her body was done.

"I can't get you what you want, Theo. I'm so very sorry," she mumbled into his neck, finally giving in and relaxing completely against him.

"Then you're about to have a pretty rough night, sweetheart." His tone was all determination with more than a hint of threat.

Chapter 4

The woman wasn't faking exhaustion. Theo carried her through his apartment to the master bedroom after driving more than an hour to get through the city. She'd fallen asleep before he'd even put her in his car.

She slept soundly against him, her small body curled against his chest. The witch brought out feelings in him he really didn't like, and he couldn't exactly blame her since all she was doing was sleeping. It was the one true time he knew she wasn't trying to manipulate him, and yet, he wanted nothing more than to protect her and keep her safe. How did she do that?

More importantly, what the hell was wrong with her? Why couldn't she create fire?

He laid her down on the bed and then sighed, looking at her sopping wet clothing while switching on the bedside lamp. "Ginny? Wake up."

She didn't even stir. Surprisingly long lashes swept down her pale cheeks, and in sleep, her pink lips were relaxed and tipped up. Even out cold, she somehow smiled as if she knew a secret.

Why he liked that, he'd never know.

All right. If he left her in the wet dress, she'd freeze all night. But he couldn't just take off her clothes. Damn it. He ran a hand through his hair, scattering soot.

He'd been with more women than he could count, but this one was one of a kind. He didn't like that. Lifting her too easily with one arm, he drew back the covers and set her on her butt, her head leaning into his stomach. His dick instantly hardened to rock. Damn it. Forcing himself to relax, he deftly untied the corset and drew it off before laying her back down and quickly covering her with the bedclothes. Her thin panties could remain on. No way was he removing those.

She murmured something and turned toward him.

He pushed her hair away from her face, noting the silky softness, even with soot in it. But the mass had dried into tumbling curls. Figured she'd have naturally curly hair. "God was kind to you, darlin'," he murmured, running a knuckle down her smooth cheek. "Way too kind."

Yet what was going on?

Her pulse beat steadily in her neck, so she was unharmed at least. She sniffed and turned the other way, revealing the darkening bruise along the other side of her face.

Anger caught him in the chest. Hard. He should've ripped the head off the witch who'd hit her. An eight-story fall wasn't bad enough. He rubbed his finger across the heated bruise. Why hadn't she healed it earlier? There had been plenty of time before she'd fallen asleep. "What aren't you telling me?" He dropped to his haunches, smoothing her hair back again.

Then he examined her neck, making sure he hadn't hurt her when he'd grabbed her. Apparently she bruised easily. His chest loosened at seeing there were no bruises on her neck.

He paused. Wait a minute. He looked closer. There were no markings on her neck. Not a one. The woman had been mated, or so he thought. There would still be a bite, even from a witch. Matings were forever...until recently. A virus had been discovered that could negate the mating bond—at least when one of the mates had passed on, as Ginny's had. She had said she'd taken the virus and could be mated again. But he'd thought... Maybe he'd been wrong.

Thinking of oddities... He moved down the bed, not far, and reached for her ankle, pulling it out of the bed while making sure to keep the rest of her covered.

A anklet of diamonds and gold spikes encircled her left ankle tightly. Leather held it together, and there didn't seem to be a clasp.

How did she get it off? He rubbed her ankle, and she moaned. He paused. What in the world? Looking closer, he could see a slight green ring around her skin.

Was she so vain she'd let her skin turn green to keep diamonds on? Or did the piece have sentimental value? Perhaps it had been from her mate.

Why that made Theo's chest hurt, he had no clue. He set her ankle back beneath the covers and turned to head for the master bathroom. After a very quick and hot shower, he was feeling more in control. Oh, he'd let her sleep tonight, but in the morning she was going to tell him everything.

He strode naked into his bedroom and drew on some sweats. She didn't stir, her breathing even and deep as she slept. He shook his head, heading into his living room and double-checking his security measures.

There was no way he could just go to sleep right now. It was nearly three in the morning, which made it midnight in northern Idaho. Hoping he wasn't making a colossal mistake, he booted up his television set, put in a series of codes, and sent out a call to the Realm Headquarters. The Realm was a coalition of witches, vampires, demons, and shifters. Its leader, vampire king Dage Kayrs, slowly took shape. "What the hell, Reese?" the king asked, his dark hair mussed and his silver eyes irritated. He stood bare to the waist with a rock-type wall behind him.

Theo winced. "Sorry. Thought you might be up."

"Are you being attacked or do you need immediate assistance?" Dage's eyes cleared.

"Ah, no." Theo dropped into a chair and rubbed his scruffy chin. He should've shaved in the shower. "I was hoping the queen was up and working." The queen was a brilliant geneticist who worked around the clock trying to cure human diseases. Of course, she was at least four or five months pregnant, so she probably needed her sleep.

"I'm up." Emma Kayrs passed near the camera and slid an arm around Dage's waist. The queen's dark hair was piled on her head, and she wore what looked like Star Trek pajamas. Her belly protruded, and she rubbed it. "How are you, Theo?"

"I'm a jerk," he said. "I shouldn't have called so late."

Dage ran a hand down Emma's arm. "I see you got out of the hotel fire safely. How is Ginny O'Toole?"

Theo's mouth gaped open. He shook his head. "How did you know?" Surely news of his night hadn't already reached Idaho.

Dage rolled his eyes.

Emma grinned. "He's the king. Don't make him say it. The. King."

Theo bit back a smile. "Oh, yeah. Well, since I have you, does a mating mark disappear when a former mate takes the virus?"

Emma's startling blue eyes brightened like they did every time anybody wanted to talk science with her. "No. Never. The bite mark stays in place." She leaned into Dage more. "But the mating brand, the ones from the Kayrs family, demons, and witches… That does disappear."

"Are you sure?" Theo asked, his mind spinning.

"Definitely." The queen nodded her head vigorously. "Why?"

Theo cleared his throat. "Because Ginny doesn't have a mark on her neck." He frowned. "Though witches don't—"

"Witches do," the queen interrupted. "All male immortals have fangs, even witches, and they bite during the mating process. If Ginny doesn't still have bite marks…"

"Then she was never mated," Theo finished, shocked he could find more anger in him than before. "I can't believe it."

Dage's eyes twinkled. "Things are about to get interesting now, aren't they?"

* * * *

Somebody was chasing her. Ginny ducked low and ran, her feet flying over the invisible ground. They were coming. After all this time, she was going to lose. God. She couldn't lose.

Theo. He would help her. He had to.

She turned a corner, suddenly surrounded by trees. Dark and high, they loomed over her, providing warning. No shelter or protection. No. She didn't get those. But warning. That was a nice change.

Something crashed into the brush behind her.

She yelped and ran harder, but the grass grew into weeds. They held her fast, not letting her move. Oh, no. It was too late. She opened her mouth and screamed.

"Whoa." Warmth and strength encircled her. "Wake up, lady. You're having a bad dream."

She jerked awake, her head hitting something hard. Pain flashed through her skull.

"Damn it," Theo said, wrapping a hand in her hair and pulling her away.

Oh. She'd hit his chin with her head. "Sorry." She reached up to rub her forehead.

"You okay?" He loosened his hold, his eyes glowing in the dim light.

She blinked. Bed. She was in bed with Theo Reese. He smelled fresh and clean and male. A shadow covered his hard jaw, and his hard cut chest was bare. Oh, goodness. Did he have any clothing on? She stilled. Did she? She looked down. Nope. "You, ah, you took my clothes off." Her heart started to race.

"They were wet and dirty." He released her hair and smoothed his hand down her arm. "I didn't look." His teeth sparkled with his grin.

She blinked. Her brain went fuzzy. The bed was soft and the sheets luxurious. The world smelled strong and good...like him. "Why, I mean how, is there a light on?"

He slowly nodded. "Bathroom light. I thought you might be confused when you awoke, so I left the light on."

Now wasn't that sweet? Her body went all mushy, and she was too relaxed to stop it. "Thank you."

"That was quite the nightmare you were having," he rumbled.

She snorted. "That was nothing, believe me."

His gaze narrowed. "Really. Do you often have horrific dreams?"

Was that a weakness? She couldn't let him get that close. "No."

His lips thinned. "I thought we already discussed lying versus telling the truth. Stop lying to me."

Her chest felt heavy. The vampire had saved her from an attack squad, and he'd brought her to his home to keep safe. Then he'd left the light on for her so she wouldn't be scared. Liars really ticked him off, apparently. "Fine, Theo. I won't lie to you again." She meant every word.

His head lifted just slightly. "Do you have nightmares often?"

That was the question he'd wanted to start with? She should move away from him, but the male was all heat, and she was still cold. "Yes."

"About what?" he murmured, his gaze searching deep.

She breathed out. "Somebody chasing me. Torturing me. Killing me." It was difficult, but she forced a smile. "Normal scary dreams, you know?"

He studied her. "Who's chasing you?"

"Everybody bad," she said softly. "In the dream, I was looking for you." Heat rose to her face, making her cheeks hurt. "I mean, after last night, when you saved me, I guess that makes sense." Could she sound any more like a wimp? The idea caught her up short. When had she wanted to look strong to him? That wasn't her skill, darn it. "Thank you for saving me last night."

"You're welcome." He rubbed a gentle finger across her aching cheekbone. "Who was after you?"

"I don't know." She lifted a shoulder and then caught the sheet before it fell off her chest. "Could be anybody." Oh, she had an idea, but with her past, it really could be anybody. When was the last time she'd been in bed with a sexy, tousled male? It had been a while. And she'd bet her last pair of high heels that she'd never been this close to anybody this masculine. "I had a crush on you. Way back when," she confessed.

His eyes flared. "Then why seduce my brother?"

She winced. "I didn't seduce your brother. We were friends, and he was halfway to the high seas when we briefly dated. We shared one kiss, and it was like kissing...*my* brother. If I had one." Memories flooded her, and she smiled. "We were so young. So silly."

"Was it a cover?" Theo asked, once again threading his fingers through her hair.

Warmth tingled over her scalp. Her breath caught. "Yes. I was in Ireland to steal the McDougall emeralds."

Theo stiffened. "That was you?"

"Aye," she said, missing her homeland all of a sudden.

"McDougall had stolen them first, which you probably already knew. I just stole them back for the original owners." A sweet little couple from way up north. They had them hidden to this day. "My da and I were a good team." Lord, she missed him. So very much. She had to succeed in this mission. No matter what.

"I'm sorry about your father. I heard he passed during the last war," Theo said quietly, caressing through her hair.

Sadness tried to take her, and she banished it, considering she wasn't telling the whole truth. "Yes. We were moving guns for the demons, and he ran afoul of some Kurjan soldiers." Then her life had taken a decidedly bad turn. "It's been ten years, and I still think he's going to call me up with a job." Of course, he wasn't really dead. But Theo didn't know that.

"What about your so-called mate?" Theo leaned in, his nose near to hers. "I know you never mated."

She brightened. "That was the only way I could get Jared to go follow his dream and be a pirate. He was so honorable. One kiss, and he thought I needed protection for life." She cleared her throat. "At first, I had a lifetime of debts to repay because of my dad's gambling. But he stopped gambling and we worked together. So breaking and entering, robbing and bribing, became, well, fun."

"Fun?" Theo growled.

"Yes." If Theo got any closer, his mouth would be on hers. Her thighs moved restlessly. Aye, she'd wondered through the years about him. Now he was so damn close. Did she have the courage to take a nip? "Let's not talk about your brother when we're in bed, Theo."

"Why not?" he asked, his voice hoarse.

"Because of this." Finally, she moved forward and kissed him.

Chapter 5

Theo's entire body jolted. His mind spun from her revelations of being a thief, a famous one, but right now his body ruled. Her soft lips worked his mouth, tentatively at first, and then with passion. Her small hands spread across his chest and over his shoulders, and she pressed into him with only the thin sheet and his old sweats as barriers.

He'd had more dreams about her than he could count. It had killed him when she'd chosen his brother to dick over instead of him. Yet he tightened his hold in her thick hair and tugged her back.

She gave a small sound of protest and then met his gaze. Passion had darkened her eyes to deep sapphire. "Theo?" she breathed.

His cock pounded with her so near. A part of him, one he didn't like, whispered to shut the hell up and take what she was offering. But she was a master with men, and he'd actually had a crush on her eons ago. "I like this new honesty thing you have going on, but I don't trust you."

Her eyes widened and then she laughed. Humor spilled from her. "Oh, that makes sense." She hummed and spread her fingers out over his shoulders. "I've never, not once, seduced a man like this."

He lifted an eyebrow.

She grinned and bit her lip. "I mean naked in bed. I've never slept with a mark or used sex." She ducked her head. "I've used wiles and promises, but never actual sex. I'm not that bad, Theo."

God, she was cute. Every nerve he owned wanted to believe her,

and his gut said she was telling the truth. His body was already hers...
He just had to protect his brain. But it was difficult with her soft skin
and sweet scent so close. Finally. He wanted inside her and now.
"Where's my file, Ginny?" he asked.

Her straight teeth played with her lip. "You can't have it. Sorry."
She sighed and released him.

Damn it. He wanted those hands back on his skin. Now. "So
you at least admit you stole it."

"Yep."

He blinked. "What game are you playing now?"

She tugged the sheet up more and wiggled around a little, as if
trying to get comfortable. Good to know he wasn't the only one
hurting. "You saved me, so no more lies. I'm not lying to you ever
again. So the truth is that I stole the file, I'm keeping it, and you can't
have it back."

Now he laughed. "Ginny, you're not the only one who's led an
interesting life."

"I know all about you, Theo." She reached out and ran a finger
down his jugular, sending shock waves through his body. "I know
what you did in the last war. Your reputation as a soldier and a
sniper. Things your brothers probably don't even know."

He frowned and leaned back. She knew about him? "Bullshit."

"They call you the Phantom. Because you can get the job done
without leaving a trace. You can also get answers." She hummed.
"The demons call you the Interrogator. Such a boring name."

Yet he'd earned both names. "Those are both stupid and don't
come close to describing actions in war." The woman wasn't the only
one with nightmares. "Apparently you've kept track of me." He
wasn't sure he liked her knowing so much about him. His secrets
were his own, damn it.

"I have," she said. "Call it curiosity."

His ego wanted to swell, and he batted it down. Hard. "If you
know about me, then you know I'll get my file back. No matter what
I have to do." He didn't want to hurt her.

She laughed again, the sound sexy and throaty. "Oh, Theo. You
couldn't torture me. Not in a million years."

He smiled. "You're right."

She paused. "Okay." Now she sounded a mite worried.

He tried not to take too much pleasure in that fact. "You're obviously on a job—probably more than one. While I won't harm you, I'm also going to prevent you from finishing any job you might be undertaking. Whoever hired you is going to be pissed because you're going to fail. Repeatedly. Until I get my file back."

Her head snapped back. "You wouldn't."

Adorable. She really was. When her temper showed, she was glorious. "I would and I will." Now he leaned in, feathering his mouth across hers. "We both know you can't throw fire, and for some reason, your strength is depleted. You can't fight me and win." He kissed her softly, taking his time, enjoying the taste of woman and the thrill of the challenge in getting his file back. "You're probably out of sedatives, baby."

Her lips pursed. "This isn't an old Hepburn and Tracy movie. I can't give your file back."

"Okay." He never lost a challenge, and she'd have to learn that the hard way. Truth be told, he liked battling her. Entirely too much. The temptation of her was too much to resist, though. So he drew her close and stopped playing, taking her mouth hard.

She moaned and moved into him, kissing him back, her tongue dueling with his. Soft and sweet, her scent surrounded him. Hot spikes of lust pierced him. He took her deeper, pulling her on top of him. The second her skin met his, he groaned. Her thighs dropped to either side of his, her sex cradling his erection.

He slid a hand down her back, pressing her closer. God. White hot lights flashed behind his eyes. He could have his sweats and her panties off in seconds.

She tunneled her hands in his hair, kissing him back, her body flush on him, her nipples tight against his chest.

He should halt this. Give it a second. Make sure it was real. But his body wouldn't stop. His mouth kissed her harder, taking control.

She gave as good as she got, as if she too knew their time together wouldn't last. They were on opposite sides.

At the thought, he pulled away.

She was spread over him, her lips rosy, a stunning flush across her face. "We should stop," she mused.

"Yes." He ran his hand down her bare back, halting at the dip at her waist. God, she felt fucking amazing. "Or we go into this with our eyes wide open."

Interest and need glimmered in her stunning eyes. "Meaning?"

He was backwoods crazy to even suggest it, but who the hell cared? "This is just this. You and me satisfying curiosity from years ago and taking the edge off. The second we're dressed and out of bed, we're on opposite sides of this thing. I'll do what I have to in order to get my file back." It was only fair to warn her.

"That's crazy," she murmured, rubbing against him.

"I know," he admitted, the blood rushing through his head to ring in his ears. "But I want you and have for centuries. You're almost naked on top of me, and it's taking every ounce of self-control I have not to roll you over and fuck you so hard you forget about the file. Until you forget about everything but me."

She swallowed and sat up on him, her full breasts bouncing. "I, ah, don't want you to think I'm easy."

His heart turned over. Hard. Damn, she was sweet when she lost the act. "We moved out of the last century a while ago, sweetheart. I don't think you're easy." He flattened his hand over her upper chest and caressed down, tweaking both her nipples. "But I might not let you go."

She gasped and leaned into him, her panties becoming wet right over his cock. "I want this, too. But you have to know that I'll fight dirty afterward." Her voice was throaty and devastatingly sexy.

"I wouldn't have it any other way." He grasped her nipples and pulled her down.

She opened her mouth on a gasp, and he took full advantage, grasping the back of her head and holding her in place. He kissed her deep, his hand tangled in her hair, his other hand kneading her nipple. Yeah. His Ginny liked a little bite with her pleasure. He'd known she'd be like this.

Sexy, hot, and responsive.

She gyrated against him, her core moving along his shaft. With a moan into his mouth, she reached down and shoved his sweats off his hips.

He helped her, using his legs to completely kick them off.

The second she settled back over him, her wet core right against his dick, he almost lost his mind. Growling, he rolled over, pressing her into the bed. Her legs spread, and her soft thighs rubbed the outside of his.

"Now, Theo," she whispered, her nails scraping down his back.

Oh, she didn't get to call the shots here. He kissed along her jawline and down, taking his time with her breasts. God, she was perfect. Whether he wanted her to be or not, she was everything he'd ever wanted. Even the thieving. The damn intrigue with her went way beyond the physical.

He was in trouble, and he didn't give a shit.

Reaching down, he snapped her panties in two. Then he kissed his way down her abdomen, noting how small her ribs really were. God, he'd have to be careful with her. Reaching her core, he licked her slit.

All woman and spice. She gasped and stiffened. He grinned, going at her, showing no mercy. Her G-spot was an easy find inside her, and he used two figures to torture her. Then he licked her clit, giving just enough pressure to have her gasping for relief. Her skin was beyond soft, and her body incredibly responsive.

"Theo," she moaned, her nails raking down his scalp.

He loved the pain. But if he didn't get inside her soon, he was going to explode. So he nipped her clit and twisted his fingers inside her wet heat. She arched into his mouth, crying out, her entire body shuddering with her release. He kept her going until she settled back with a whimper.

Then he moved up her body, kissing and licking, finally reaching her mouth. "You are so sweet," he murmured.

She grinned and shoved him over, rolling on top of him again. "Remember that when I kick your ass later." Aroused, having fun, her brogue emerged.

Just one more sexy thing about the woman.

"I'll keep that in mind." He could feel her pulsing clit along his dick. "You sure about this?"

"Definitely." She leaned over and then paused. Her eyes widened. She stiffened and pulled back.

He blinked. "Ginny?"

"Oh." She scrambled back, her face losing all color. "What time is it?" She looked around, her gaze frantic.

He grabbed her biceps to keep her from falling onto the floor. "It's only about six in the morning." He tried to slow his heart rate, but her bare breasts were right in front of his face. Pretty pink nipples and full globes that already carried whisker burn from him. "What's wrong?"

She shoved off him, standing and weaving, pale in her nudity. "Oh, God. It's after five." She looked around. "Where's my laptop bag?"

"In the other room." He sat up, confusion mixing with anger. She was too pale. Way too pale. "What's going on?"

"I need my phone," she hissed, suddenly crying out. "Damn it." She hopped on one foot, panic cascading from her. "In my bag. Get my phone."

He looked down at her lifted ankle with the band around it. "What the hell is that thing?"

She cried out again, grabbing the anklet and falling to the ground. "Please, Theo. Get me the phone." Purple striations rose from her ankle up to her knee.

He launched into the other room, finding her cell phone in her laptop bag and hurrying back with it.

She held it, tears streaming down her face as she made a quick text. Then she cried out again, clutched her ankle to her body, and passed out cold.

Chapter 6

Ginny came to surrounded by softness and the scent of…Theo. Her eyelids flashed open to see his dark eyes filling her world.

"You alive?" he asked, his hair tousled as he leaned over her, his big hand on her forehead. "I admit I give a hell of an orgasm."

"Aye." She glanced around. Apparently Theo had pulled a big T-shirt over her head before setting her back in the bed. She pushed herself up to sit, shoving her hair away from her face. "So."

He sat on the bed, wearing worn sweats and a frown. His big and broad chest beckoned her to take a bite, but warning all but rolled from him. "You have three minutes to explain what's happening, or I take off that anklet." He jerked his head toward a knife he'd placed on the bedside table. "I'm assuming it's made of phanekite."

"Planekite," she corrected. "Well, it depends who you talk to in what you call it. But yes. It's made of the one mineral in the world that can harm witches." The damn stuff could kill them, and at the moment, enemies had made darts full of the stuff. But her anklet was old school.

He reached for the knife. Determination and what appeared to be fury pounded a muscle beneath his jaw. "I don't even want to know why you're continuing to wear that. Let's take it off, and then you're going to tell me all about who put it there."

She held up a hand. "It's rigged. You cut it, and spikes slash into my skin, filling me with planekite. A lethal dose."

He paused, his eyes somehow darkening even more. "Let me get this straight. The thing is made of planekite, which obviously weakens you until you can't throw fire. It can be remotely controlled to jolt you with doses, which is what I just saw happen." He grasped her hand, his gentle touch completely opposed to the rage glittering in those eyes. "And if you try to remove it, the thing is booby trapped to kill you."

"Yes," she breathed, her shoulders relaxing. It felt so damn good to talk about the anklet. She'd had to keep it secret for so long.

"Who?" Theo asked, his jaw looking harder than a boulder.

She shouldn't say. But the heaviness of keeping the burden to herself was overwhelming. It was too much. "Saul Libscombe," she whispered.

"Goddamn motherfucker." Theo pushed away from her, standing and facing the doorway, fury vibrating the muscles in his back. "This is *our* fault?"

"No." Ginny spread her hands out on the bedclothes. "It's my fault. I'm a thief, and that life catches up to you."

He pivoted so quickly to face her that she lost her breath. "My family has been at odds with the Libscombes for years. We killed them, they killed us, and now Saul is the only one left standing. He did this to you so you'd get to us."

"Aye." Things had gotten a lot worse the last month when Jared Reese had killed Petey Libscombe, who was Saul's brother. But the Reese family had probably thought things were over, since Saul appeared to be the one good shifter in his family. The guy had a good front but was more evil than the rest put together. Ginny plucked at a loose string. "Saul has been playing the long game, while Petey kept you off balance the last few years. Saul wanted the Benjamin file, and I'm the only one who could get close enough to steal it. I'm so sorry, Theo."

"Long game?" Everything around Theo stilled, as if gathering for an explosion. "How long have you worn that fucking thing?"

She bit her lip.

"Ginny?" His voice went dangerously low.

"Ten years," she whispered, preparing for him to detonate.

He didn't move. Didn't even twitch. "Ten. Years."

She nodded, her heart beating too fast for her to ease. He was scaring the hell out of her, and that wasn't easy to do. "This has been a campaign full of movements, including stealing a lot of gold. He's been setting it up for a decade, and now he's made his move. I'm sorry."

"Why didn't you come to me?" Theo whispered, lines cutting edges into the side of his mouth.

Her heart took a hit. He would've helped her. She could see that now. "You didn't like me." She cleared her throat, going full in. "And he has my father somewhere. Da is still alive."

Theo rocked back. "He has your dad."

She nodded. "Even if I could get the anklet off, the second I do, my dad is dead."

Theo moved for her and dropped to his haunches, gingerly taking her ankle in his hands. His broad hands could easily snap the anklet in two, but he just examined it. "There must be sensors here somewhere."

"Aye." While there was no good way out of this mess, her shoulders finally relaxed from around her ears. She wasn't alone. Finally. No matter what happened, she had Theo with her for this moment. Actually on her side. She smiled. "If I give Saul the file, the anklet comes off and my dad goes free."

Theo cocked his head to the side, and his gaze traveled to meet hers. "Ah, sweetheart. You don't believe that, do you?"

She pressed her lips together. "About the anklet? No. But I won't hand over the file until my dad is free. That's my only goal."

"I'm gonna kill your dad when this is over." Theo lifted her leg until the anklet was at eye level. He studied it for several moments. "I can't believe he made you a thief."

"I'm a great thief," she said, giving in to temptation and feeling along his jawline. Firm and solid. Yeah. That was Theo. "Da and I only stole from bad people or from people who didn't need what they had. We've financed some wonderful charities throughout the ages, and we've done some good."

"You enjoy it." Theo set her leg down and rocked back, studying her. "The thieving."

"Sometimes." Why lie about it? "I've helped a lot of people."

"You're a thief." He shook his head and stood, withdrawing.

Oh, yeah. She'd forgotten that side of Theo Reese. The honorable, law-abiding, honest guy. What he'd done as a soldier, he'd done during war. Some people didn't realize that wars always went on...just not publicly. "I am." She wouldn't lie to him again. "Don't get me wrong. I'd love to work full time for a nonprofit like Other Tracks. Do real work and get some good done." She gestured toward the anklet. "But that's not going to be my path, and we both know it."

"You're giving up?"

"No. Just being realistic." She slid to the edge of the bed. "Now I need a shower, and then I have to meet Saul."

Theo crossed his arms, his gaze implacable. "Oh, lady. Your entire life just changed. Accept that now."

Her head snapped up, and she stood. In her bare feet, looking up at least a foot to his hard gaze, she barely held back a telltale shiver. "Excuse me?"

"You've been tagged like an animal to get to me and my family." His arms uncrossed. "You stole a file that could ruin us." He moved toward her and took both arms in his, lifting her up on her toes. "You just became my responsibility, whether you like it or not. Get on board and now."

* * * *

Theo kept his gaze stoic when all he wanted to do was punch a wall. To think she'd lived with this pain for an entire decade without anybody to help her. That ended and right now.

Her gaze softened. "You can't save me, Theo."

The fuck he couldn't. "Take a shower. We'll talk after you're feeling better." His doorbell rang, and he released her.

She jerked. "Who's here?"

"Reinforcements. I called my brothers the second I recognized the planekite. Shower. Now." He turned her and patted her ass to get her going. She slapped his hand. Good. Her spunk was coming back. "You have five minutes and I'm dragging you out of there."

She paused at the doorway and flipped him off.

He grinned and grabbed her suitcase to drop outside the bathroom. Then he headed for his front door, bypassing his sprawling living room with the quiet brick fireplace. Reaching the front door, he opened it just as Jared was about to bust through. "Geez. Give me a minute."

His brothers both stomped inside, brushing snow off their leather jackets. Jared had black hair and even blacker eyes, while Chalton had blond hair and black eyes and much more angular features. They were both about Theo's height at six-foot-five, and right now wore matching frowns.

"She has a planekite band on her ankle?" Jared snarled, slamming the door behind himself.

"Yes. She's worn it for a decade and is now being blackmailed to hurt us," Theo said, jerking his head at the computer bag over Chalton's shoulder. "Did you bring anything that will help?"

Chalton shrugged. "I don't know. Let's take a look at the anklet." As the computer genius for the entire Realm, Chalton had the best equipment. "Though aren't you the one who hacked me last month?"

"I am." Theo grinned, unable to help himself, warming that his brothers had come immediately to help. It was good to be back in each other's lives after too long of a time. "But I don't have the hardware the Realm is using. You have it."

Chalton nodded. "Fair enough."

Jared ran a hand through his shaggy hair, taking note of Theo's bare chest. "Anything you want to tell us?"

"No." Theo gestured them into the living room, with its dark sofas, before pressing a button on the wall. The blinds lifted to reveal the New York skyline just coming awake.

"I can smell her on you," Chalton muttered, sitting and unpacking his bag. He looked toward Jared. "Is this going to be weird?"

Jared dropped into a leather chair. "Theo is always weird." He scrubbed both hands down his face. "I wasn't in love with her, and now I know that fact since I've mated Veronica. But I do like Ginny, and I hate that she's been used against us like this."

"Me too." Theo rolled his neck and remained standing. "Saul is coming after us." God. He had to keep the Green Rock file away from Chalton. Jared had known about the file way back when, but Chalton needed to be protected. "Has anybody heard from Uncle Benny?"

Jared exhaled loudly. "Yes. He's coming home from Russia to kill us. If we go quietly, he'll leave Mom alone."

Chalton winced. "All we did was blow up two of his homes and get his private data stolen. Does that require death?"

"Yes," Theo and Jared said in unison. They weren't kidding, either. Theo looked around his high-end place. "Is there anything we could offer Benny?"

"Just our heads," Jared said grimly.

Damn it. Spare him from thousand-year-old vampires who just couldn't relax and find humor in a good explosion. "One thing at a time," Theo said. "When Saul attacked Ginny through the anklet earlier, she texted him that she'd meet him at rendezvous point B tomorrow at midnight. So I'm guessing it's somewhere she has to travel to reach."

"Guessing?" Jared sat back, his gaze narrowing. "She hasn't told you?"

Theo crossed his arms. "She's not going to trust us completely, especially with her dad's life, until we show we can help. She's been on her own a long time, Jar."

Jared coughed. "Her dad is alive?"

"Yes, and he's imprisoned by Saul." Theo's hands clenched into fists. "I can't believe she's dealt with this by herself for a fucking decade."

Jared and Chalton exchanged a look.

"What?" Theo asked, his instincts humming.

Chalton shrugged, typing rapidly on his computer. "You've always had a thing for her. I remember centuries ago… And you liked her."

"So?" Theo asked.

Jared grinned. "It's fun to see you be the one dangling after the last several months. You had many a smart-ass comment when Chalton and I were, ah…"

"Turning into mated wussies?" Theo asked, matching his grin.

Jared rolled his eyes. "Yeah. That."

"Listen." Theo had never lied to his brothers, and he wasn't going to start now. "I like her, but this is just temporary and to scratch a quick itch. The woman is a thief, and she'll be gone when we're done here."

Charlton snorted.

Jared coughed into his hand.

Theo rolled his eyes. "Whatever. Just because you guys got all domesticated doesn't mean I will. Come on." Even as he said the words, they sounded hollow to him. He was spared whatever retort his brothers wanted to make by Ginny moving into the room.

With her wet hair curling down her back, sans the makeup, she looked about eighteen. Pure and innocent except for the sparkle in those dangerously blue eyes. Unlike her usual fitted dress, she'd pulled on faded jeans with a soft robin's egg blue sweater. The bruise from the night before marred her right cheek with an odd purple, making her look both beautiful and tragic.

She smiled. "The Reese boys all in one place." With an exaggerated movement, she winked at Theo. "I hope your apartment is insured."

Chapter 7

Ginny moved into the room, feeling like a doe surrounded by hungry panthers. The Reese boys en masse managed to take over the very atmosphere with a sense of male power. Even among vampires, they had presence. Their closeness was obvious, and she clasped her hands together as she sat in a leather seat. "Rumor has it Uncle Benny is heading home."

"Yes," Jared said, his gaze on her bruise. "Who hurt you?" His brows drew down.

She touched the still aching cheekbone. "An idiot Theo threw out a window afterward." She smiled.

"You can't heal yourself?" Chalton asked gently.

She shook her head. "The anklet keeps my powers at bay, unfortunately." Could this be any more awkward? She'd dated Jared, kind of played him a little, had stolen from their family, and now had orgasmed from Theo's very talented mouth. Heat flushed into her cheeks, and she couldn't stop the blush.

Theo swore under his breath and moved for her, plucking her out of the chair and sitting back down with her in his lap. "Relax, lady. Jared forgives you for the past, Chalton isn't mad about the Benjamin file, and you and I are working together until we're not. Same rules as before."

Humor filled Jared's eyes. "He's given you rules?"

She snorted and rolled her eyes. "He likes rules, you know?"

Chalton nodded, his gaze on his screen as he typed. "Always has been a tightass."

That easily, she relaxed into Theo's heat. They were friends again. At least for now. "I'm sorry I can't give you the file back," she said, her chest starting to hurt.

"We'll get it back," Theo said easily. "Let's worry about one thing at a time."

She nodded. "Jared, I'm sorry in general."

The eldest Reese brother gave her a grin. "It's all good, Gin. Though my Veronica feels terrible you two got into a fistfight while you were hampered by the anklet. She would've never hit you had she known."

Ginny laughed. "That's a 'nice to meet you' among my people. I like your mate. Very much."

He smiled. "I'll let her know. Just so you know, you and I are friends and always will be. Even when you toss Theo out on his ass."

She could read people, and if she was reading Jared right, he was greatly amused by something. Was it Theo and her? That was silly. They were temporary and would soon be on opposing sides again. "Um, okay."

Chalton stopped typing. "Can I see the anklet?"

She nodded and stretched out her bare foot, planting it on the coffee table and pulling up her jeans leg.

Chalton leaned forward, took a look, and then started typing. "Since it can be activated remotely, it sends out waves. Let me see what I can find out."

Ginny nodded, allowing Theo to pull her back into his heat. She settled against him, trying not to dream about what it'd feel like to have somebody all the time. To be with Theo all the time. He made her feel safe and protected, and that couldn't last. Yet she snuggled into him anyway, letting him hold her. If she let her heart be broken by him, it was her own fault. And the ride might just be worth it.

Chalton sat back, his gaze on the screen.

"Well?" Theo asked, his breath brushing Ginny's ear.

She shivered and cuddled closer. "It can't be deactivated, right?"

Chalton nodded, his full mouth turning down. He always had been the quiet one in the family.

She turned to face Theo's dark eyes, her stomach churning. "I appreciate your trying to help, but I researched this thing extensively when it was first forced on me. It can't be removed, and the only way to deactivate it is at its source. Where Saul has it."

"She's correct," Chalton said. "The technology is as good as anything we have. Saul must've spent decades perfecting it."

Theo's face remained calm, but anger poured from him to surround her. She patted his bare chest. "It's okay. It really is."

"It's not okay," he gritted out. "Where is Saul? Let's take him out now."

"I don't know," she sighed. "Believe me, if I knew where he was and where he has my da, I would've hired an attack force years ago. But he's remained under the radar."

Realization dawned in Theo's eyes. "Until you actually stole the file. Now he has to meet you to get it."

She nodded, her gaze dropping to his mouth. "Yes. I can't wait much longer. The anklet is taking too much of a toll, and I don't know when it'll be too late for me to move against him."

"What was your real plan?" Theo pushed her curling hair away from her face, his touch infinitely gentle even with the anger glowing so brightly in his dark eyes.

"Steal the file, get my dad released, kill Saul." She was enjoying Theo's touch entirely too much.

Jared sighed. "It's not a bad plan except for the last part. Saul will be expecting an attack."

Theo nodded. "Yeah, but he won't be expecting us to be part of it."

Hope flared inside her. Hot and bright. "You'll help me take out Saul?"

"Yes, but not with the file," Theo said. "We have to find another way."

Of course. His family had to come first with him. She understood that. Forcing a smile, she made herself nod. "Okay. That makes sense."

His gaze narrowed. "Don't try to play me."

She had no choice. "I'm not." Why the hell was he so tough to fool? Her eyelids fluttered. "I need some protein to combat the planekite. Maybe some Vitamin C?" She'd found that oranges and turkey bacon had actually helped somewhat on more than one occasion. Almonds as well.

"Where's the file, Ginny?" Theo asked.

She dropped the pretense. "I'm sorry." Her phone rang in her back pocket, and she jumped.

Theo pulled it out before she could and read the face. His face went blank, and he pressed the speaker button. "Answer," he mouthed.

She glared and then shoved him in the gut. "Hello?"

Theo put the phone down on the coffee table.

"So glad to hear you survived the reminder this morning," Saul said, his voice nasally over the line. "You know what happens when you don't check in."

"Where's my da?" she returned, trying desperately to ignore the tension suddenly choking the room.

Saul chuckled. "You'll see him soon. But I needed to see what you're up to now. Your GPS puts you at Theo Reese's apartment in New York. I knew you'd do anything for a job, but Theo Reese?"

Theo's body somehow hardened around her. Only her training kept her voice from shaking. "Did you send the attack squad last night?" What was she dealing with here?

Saul sighed. "Yes. You've been so difficult to work with about the Benjamin file, so I thought we'd just take it."

"I don't have it with me, you moron." She shook her head. Saul really was an idiot. "More than that, you created the situation I'm in right now. Theo was angry I took the file you wanted, he defended me from your goons, and now he's threatening to keep me under lock and key until he gets it back. I told you he'd be a problem." She gave the man in question a hard look.

He merely lifted an eyebrow.

The line crackled. "Where is Theo now?" Saul asked.

"In the shower, Saul," she answered, forcing boredom into her voice.

"Well now, I knew you were a loose bitch," Saul snapped.

Theo growled low, and she shoved him in the stomach. The man had to be quiet, damn it. "Just because I turned you down, Saul, doesn't mean I like to go to bed lonely." She couldn't help get the dig in.

Pain flared along her ankle, and she cried out.

Theo vibrated, reaching for the anklet, determination hardening his jaw.

She quietly slapped him away. The poison entered her bloodstream, just a small dose, and her limbs went numb. Her head lolled. "That the best you've got?"

Saul laughed. "Oh, you and I are going to have some fun together once you give me that file. I'll let your father go, but you and I aren't finished. Got it?"

"You and I never got started, remember?" She wasn't going to let the asshole have any illusions. "I said no."

"That was before you'd worn a planekite anklet for years," he said slowly. "If you want that off, you'll do whatever I tell you to do, or we both know it's going to kill you. The long-term effects can't be healthy. My guess? You'll need to mate to regain your strength."

What a complete bastard. She was going to kill him, and she was going to enjoy seeing him bleed first. "Planekite is preferable to you, asshole." She waited for the blast to her ankle, but one didn't come.

"I'm offering to mate you and take off the ankle bracelet," he said easily. "I'm a shifter, you're a witch, and we would make powerful offspring. It might be your only chance at survival."

Bile rose in her throat. "One of us is going to die before that happens. I hope it's you." She meant every word. In fact, if she was going to die, so was he. For ten years she'd practiced fighting with a knife, just in case.

"Keep up your strength. You need to be free of Reese by tomorrow night to make it to our meeting spot," Saul snapped.

She eyed Theo. "Not a problem. He's strong but not the sharpest tool in the shed."

He lifted his chin, his lip quirking.

The phone went dead.

She breathed out, her body aching from the planekite.

"Where's the meet?" Theo asked.

She leaned her cheek against his chest. Just for the moment to regain her strength.

Theo tucked her close, his chin rubbing her forehead. "How did he get the band on you, darlin'?"

Sleepy. She was so damn sleepy. The planekite worked against her organs, making them fight hard just to do their jobs. "Attack squad of twelve. I gave a good fight, but…" She'd ended up with the ankle bracelet from hell.

Theo kissed her forehead. "I'll gut him for you, Gin. Naval to neck, I'll slice him open, yank out his guts, and stomp all over them."

Now wasn't that sweet? She actually loved the predatory vampire Theo kept carefully banked way down deep. "Are you courting me?" she whispered, trying to hide her grin.

"Maybe." Theo's breath stirred her hair, smelling like peppermint. "If I am, whatever you're planning just became my plan. Only one of us is fighting Saul hand-to-hand, and it's not the one of us hampered by a planekite anklet."

Just when he was sounding reasonable, he turned all male on her. She sighed. "Maybe it's better we didn't—"

"Don't finish that thought," he warned, his mouth next to her ear. "We are nowhere near done with what we started earlier. Once you're healthy, we're taking some time. Some serious time."

What the heck did that mean? She opened her mouth to ask, but she couldn't find the right words. Just what did Theo want from her? Other than the Benjamin file, of course.

"I've got Saul," Chalton said, his gaze on the computer. "Traced the call."

Her head snapped up. Man. She'd forgotten there were other Reese men in the room. Wait a minute. They couldn't trace Saul. She had to meet him. "What did you do?" she whispered.

Chapter 8

After supper, Theo kept an eye on the pacing woman, noting the blazing anger in her eyes. Man, she was gorgeous when riled. The New York skyline behind her didn't do her justice. He kicked back on the sofa, his feet extended onto the coffee table. He had finally gotten some food into her, and the protein had seemed to help. "I wish you'd relax," he said. Again. It had been a long damn day.

She whirled on him. "If you go after Saul, he'll have my father killed."

"No, he won't," Theo returned. Again. "We'll take him, torture him a little, and tell him that if he doesn't let your dad go, he dies. After he releases you from that damn anklet."

She shook her hair, and curls tumbled down her entire back. "He's not that dumb, Theo. Listen to me. This won't work."

He tried for patience. Truly, he did. The woman had been terrorized by this asshole, and she had a right to be frightened. His brothers were out preparing for the raid, and he'd spent the morning and afternoon gaining intel on Saul, his land holdings, and planekite. "We have confirmation that Saul is staying across town. He's *here*, Ginny. But you already knew that, didn't you?"

She had the grace to blush.

He nodded toward his laptop. "The king sent me all the Realm documentation on Saul. I know everything about the bastard now, including the fact that he owns a home two hours out of the city—where we traced his call. But still, I don't understand. Since your meet is set for somewhere in the city, or at least in this state, why wait?"

"Because Saul is supposed to bring my da from wherever he's being kept," she said. "I don't release the flash drive until I see my father get in a car and drive away." She swallowed. "Apparently Saul needed time to bring Dad here." Her chin lifted. "It's a good plan."

Theo narrowed his gaze. "Yeah. It's a great plan if we're all on board with you sacrificing yourself. I'm not, and I'm sure your father isn't, either."

Her shoulders slumped. "That's our only option, *T*."

T. He'd wondered if she remembered how she used to call him that. A lifetime ago, when they'd been friends. Man, he'd missed her. To think of the years he'd spent being angry with her while not even truly knowing her. "You're not a lamb, baby." He wasn't going to sacrifice her. Ever.

"I'm sick." She looked down at her ankle. "The planekite has infected me. There's no going back." She shrugged, her jaw firming with the stubborn tilt he somehow knew well. "This is my last chance to save my father, and I'm taking it. You have to step down."

"I think you're right about the planekite poisoning," Theo said, gesturing toward the laptop he'd pushed to the side. "The queen sent me all the research data she has on the mineral, and long-term exposure seems to be fatal. It also explains why you can't create fire or even heal the bruise on your face." Every time he looked at the dark mark, he got pissed off.

She cut him a look. "Don't sugarcoat it."

"Not going to." He leaned back and clasped his hands behind his neck, stretching his torso. "I said no lying between us, remember?"

She shoved curls out of her face. "You surely did. So yes. I'm dying. Yay for the truth."

Wasn't she cute when she was dramatic? If he told her that, she'd no doubt punch him in the face. So he went for more truth. "So we need to get mated, then."

She reared up to argue more, stopping suddenly. Her pink lips opened in an *O*. She closed them, her mouth moved again, and nothing came out.

He bit back a grin. So much for the woman leaping into his arms with gratitude. "Gin?"

Her lids half-lowered, and she pressed her hands against her hips. "You are not funny."

"I am not kidding." He wanted her more than he'd ever wanted another woman in his long life. He liked her. Hell. He wanted to be with her. It made sense on so many levels. A voice in the back of his head laughed wildly, and he banished it.

She shook her head in an odd convulsion of denial. "You've lost your damn mind, then."

"Probably," he agreed.

She swung her arms out. "We can't get mated. That's crazy. We can barely get along."

"We get along just fine," he countered. "At least we will after you give me back the information that could destroy my entire family."

"I'm a thief," she snapped, very nice color filling her face.

He nodded. "I'd very much like for you to find another profession after we mate. Definitely after we procreate." There were plenty of legal ways to help other people.

"Procreate?" she asked, her voice trembling. "Theo, you're an old-fashioned guy."

"Exactly. Arranged matings are very old fashioned," he said easily. "I spoke with the queen after she sent me the information. She agrees. The only way for you to survive this is to mate an immortal, and not another witch. You'd poison him, most likely." He sat up. "Did you know that Brenna Dunne mated Jase Kayrs, the queen's brother-in-law, for the very same reason? Because of planekite poisoning? A long time ago." He lowered his chin. "Mating a vampire saved Brenna. It will save you, too."

* * * *

Ginny couldn't breathe. Not from the planekite, but from the vampire watching her so intently. He'd dressed in casual jeans and a dark T-shirt for the day, but there was nothing casual about him. Oh, his feet were on the coffee table, and his body was stretched on the sofa, but he was all predator, ready to lunge. She could *feel* the animal in him. "Theo, you really need to stop and think about this." Her voice shook, but she couldn't help it. The mere idea of mating Theo Reese stole her breath and slid heat through her entire body.

"This is your only option for survival. I like the idea of an arranged mating spelled out with a contract," he said evenly.

Her head jerked up. "I'm sure one of your terms is the damn flash drive."

"That's a different deal. If I get your father back, you give me the flash drive." Theo's head lifted in an oddly threatening way. "Fair?"

That did sound fair through the buzzing between her ears. What was happening? Theo wanted to mate her? He was the one guy in the universe she hadn't been able to manipulate. What kind of a mating would that lead to? "You want honesty," she whispered.

"I demand it." He cocked his head to the side, studying her. "You need it."

Oh, he did not get to tell her what she needed. "You don't trust me."

"Sure, I do. You tell the truth when you agree to do so." He leaned forward, his hands clasped between his knees. "And when you lie, I can tell."

"I don't like that about you," she burst out.

He chuckled and stretched to his feet. "I'm sure. But would you really want a mate you could easily manipulate?"

Well, no. She had to admit, she respected the guy. He was smart, strong, and sexy... And he definitely knew how to kiss. But he kept her so damn off-kilter. That couldn't be good, could it? She shook her head. "Theo, mating might save me. What do you get out of it? We both know you hadn't planned on mating for a very long time."

"I've already been alive for a very long time," he countered. "I'm not a heart and flowers type of guy, Gin. Never have been. Both of my brothers are mated, and they're happy. We're a family again. A mate fits quite well into my plans."

Well then. Undying love and all of that. She breathed out. "I-I just don't know about this."

He nodded. "I understand, but it's happening, so get on board."

Wh-What? She coughed. "Theo."

"I'm not gonna let you die, sweetheart. It's that simple." He pressed a button on the computer, and something sounded from the office next to his massive kitchen. "The king said he'd be happy to negotiate on your behalf. I've just printed out my initial offer. Please take a look at it and let me know what you think."

Fire swept her. "I don't need anybody to negotiate for me. You want to negotiate? Fine. Let's do so right now." The very nerve of the males. Hell. She'd negotiated land deals that had transferred power through dynasties before.

"Okay. My offer is mating and marriage, if you want marriage. No more stealing. We live here for a couple months a year so I can see my family, and anywhere else you might want the rest of the year. I'm a soldier in contract with the Realm, so I might need to leave for work once in a while. My other business interests can be handled from anywhere." He rolled his neck, his gaze not leaving hers. "I do the fights to the death, and you can do everything else you want. Oh, and I'd like children. Someday."

There was something almost sweet about his logical approach. Which was why there was only one answer. "No."

His gaze narrowed. "That wasn't one of your options."

She sighed. "I'm not mating for convenience, and I like you way too much to see you do that. There's too much to life. To passion and maybe love. I'll take my chances when I get the anklet off." Her smile came naturally this time. "But thank you for the offer. It means the world to me." But she needed more. Especially from Theo Reese. That realization hit her so hard she nearly stumbled.

His phone buzzed, and he lifted it from his back pocket to read the face. "We're going at midnight. There's no sign of your father at Saul's New York location, but I promise I'll get the information from that bastard. You're going to have to trust me."

She glanced at the antique clock on the mantel. They had three hours before he put himself in danger. There were so many words she wanted to say, but none of them really mattered. So she moved around the sofa and stepped into his arms. "I do, Theo. But don't underestimate Saul. He's been planning this for a while."

"I won't." Theo clasped his hands at the back of her waist, pulling her tight against what felt like steel. "We are getting mated,

Gin. I'll give you a couple of days to come to terms, but I'm only negotiating on the small stuff. The bigger decision has been made."

"No," she said softly.

"I'll just have to change your mind." Without giving her warning, his mouth took hers. He lifted her, turning and walking toward the bedroom.

She wrapped her arms around his neck, holding tight, her thighs hugging his hips. Liquid lava poured through her veins, catching her off guard. Hunger shook her, shooting through her. How did he do that? She kissed him back, and suddenly cold air brushed her bare skin as he removed her shirt.

He managed to toss her bra wherever her shirt had landed, and she didn't care. "God, you're beautiful," he murmured, kissing along her neck. "That's not why, Gin."

She bit his jaw. "Not why what?"

He leaned back, desire glittering in his eyes. "Your beauty. I do like it, but it's your spirit that calls to me. Your attitude and your brains. Those turn me on even more than your unbelievably stunning eyes."

Everything in her softened.

He released her, letting her slide down his body. "I'm not good with the mushy words, but I want this. I want you. Forever."

She blinked. Those were great mushy words. "We're rushing this."

"Your survival is more important than time," he said, running his hands down her sides. "Say yes. Please let me save you."

It hit her then. Harder than any punch ever had. She wanted him. Had for centuries. When she saw her heart, when she daydreamed, it had always been him. But he hadn't mentioned love. Didn't even consider it. What better way to fall in love than to be mated? She could be what he wanted. They could find love.

She lifted her chin and met his gaze. The challenge of Theo Reese was hers to accept. "Yes."

Chapter 9

Everything inside Theo settled. Right then and there. She said yes. "You won't regret it." He'd spend a lifetime making sure of it—after he saved her life. He slid his hand up her back to capture her nape, leaning down to kiss her.

His damn phone buzzed again. Swearing, he reached for it, reading the face. "Shit. Saul ordered a car at eleven." He stepped back, his mind going into battle mode. "We have to go now." Somebody banged on his door. "Coming." He set Ginny to the side. "Get dressed, Gin." He hustled out, shutting the door and jogging through the living room to the front door. At this point, he was never going to get inside the woman.

He yanked open his front door.

Jared and Chalton moved in, already shrugging into bulletproof vests. "Where the hell would he be going tonight?" Jared muttered, handing over a vest.

"Who knows?" Theo fastened the Velcro and then moved over to remove a long painting of an island that no longer existed in the Arctic. He planted his hand flat against the wall, and it slid open to reveal a small room holding a multitude of weapons. He stepped inside and started handing out guns and knives, already knowing his brothers' preferences.

Ginny poked her head around the corner. "That's a nice Fremt."

He nodded and slid the green laser gun into the back of his waist. Lasers turned to solid bullets when impacting immortal flesh.

"I don't plan to use it. I'm better with a knife." He didn't want her to see this side of him, but maybe it was necessary. When they mated, they'd need to let each other in to their hidden worlds. "I've called for Realm soldiers to guard the door and exits to the building here," he said, partly for her comfort and partly to warn her. "You're to stay safe."

She rolled her eyes. "I have the flash drive, which keeps me safe from Saul. You're the one running into danger."

"I'm glad we already have our roles straight," he said, enjoying the instant swirling temper in her eyes.

Jared cut him a curious look, but he didn't respond. So Jared finished suiting up and headed back out. "I'll make sure the guards are at post out here." He disappeared with Chalton on his heels.

Theo inserted a couple more knives along his right leg. "I'm sorry about earlier." They kept getting interrupted.

She smiled. "That's all right. We were both carried away. This is probably better."

He stood to his full height. "It's a done deal, Gin. There's no other alternative for you, and you know that deep down. Don't worry. We'll make it work." He grasped her and kissed her hard. "Stay here." Without waiting for an answer, he moved into the hallway to follow his brothers down to transport.

He fully intended to end Saul Libscombe for good.

* * * *

Ginny's mind spun, but she had to focus. The second Theo had departed, she moved toward his computer and read all the data from the queen. Her stomach turned queasy, but she forced herself to read the Realm notes. They were in line with what she'd already learned by research and by living with the damn anklet for the past ten years.

It had already killed her.

Well, if she didn't mate. She'd meant it when she'd said yes to Theo.

Could they make it work? Maybe if they ever actually made it to bed, they had a chance. She grinned and closed the computer file. Another one caught her eye, and she didn't hesitate to click on it.

Oh, she'd been studying Saul Libscombe for a decade, so she didn't expect to find many revelations in Theo's compilation. And yet, there was some new information there. "Look at that," she breathed, taking note of a safety deposit box right there in the city, as well as some land holdings he had in Russia. Of course, Theo's contacts in Russia were far better than hers. But how in the world had he found a safety deposit box she'd missed?

Squinting, she leaned forward and read the name of the bank. Oh. It was a Realm bank here in the city. No wonder she hadn't found it. The Realm was notoriously secretive. And yet, vampires helped vampires. The king had obviously sent this file to Theo. The land didn't interest her.

But the deposit box. Now that held promise.

Of course, she'd already known of several places Saul had stashed information and funds throughout the world, but she hadn't been able to make a move because of the GPS in the anklet.

Saul would be busy with the Reese brothers tonight. If she was ever going to make a move against him, it would have to be tonight before everything went to hell. If Theo's plan didn't work, Saul would set off her anklet. Now was her one chance to get him. To maybe find leverage to use.

She chewed her thumbnail, thinking. It wasn't like she'd vowed to stay in the apartment. No. Theo had just ordered her to stay, and he'd assumed she would. She'd never been a soldier, but she knew how to broker information. Breaking into a Realm bank was colossally crazy, and yet... Whatever Saul had secured there had to be good. He was a shifter, not a vampire. For a shifter to use a Realm bank, he must really want to keep something under wraps.

Reaching for her phone, she dialed up one of her many contacts.

"Phil's Brewery," said a chipper female voice.

"Hey, Sally. It's Ginny," she said evenly.

A series of clicks came over the line. Then, "Hey, girlfriend! It's been so long since I've heard from you. What's up?" Sally asked.

Ginny grinned. "So much I don't have time to tell you right now, but we'll catch up soon." The thousand-year-old witch was one of her favorite people in life. Plus, she had skills. "I need the schematics for the Realm Bank in New York City."

Sally tsked her tongue. "Are you crazy? Even you aren't insane enough to rob Dage Kayrs."

Ginny bit her lip. That was a damn good point. "I didn't say I was robbing him. I just want the bank schematics." It wasn't like the king owned the box she was going to break into. "Besides, Dage is a friend." Okay. Not her friend. But he was obviously close to Chalton.

"Then why not just ask him to let you into his bank?" Sally asked reasonably.

Ginny shut her eyes. "Because he might say no." The guy probably had contracts with people who used the safety deposit boxes, right? "I don't want to put him in a tough position."

Sally laughed high and loud. "You are still so full of blarney. I have the schematics, but they're going to cost you. A lot."

Ginny sighed. "I'm sure. Email them to me, and I'll send secured payment immediately."

"Triple my usual price," Sally said, her voice deepening with the pleasure of a good deal.

Ginny winced. "Fair enough. And if I get caught, I know the drill." She had no clue where the schematics came from.

"All right, doll. Watch your email." Sally clicked off.

Ginny waited for the beep and then sent almost her entire savings account across the world. If this worked, it'd be worth it. She stood and stretched. If Theo had the doors covered, she'd have to figure another way out of the building.

She couldn't help but smile as she got to work. If she did this right, she'd take down Saul, and she'd be home before Theo walked through the door.

What could possibly go wrong?

* * * *

Theo crouched down in the snow after taking out the guard nearest the back door. The drive to Saul's had taken more than two hours because of the damn weather. A snowstorm barreled around Theo, turning the world white and hard to see. He stepped over the unconscious shifter guard and moved silently for the window to the east. Libscombe's New York home was on two acres in the middle of a high-end subdivision complete with gate, guardhouse, and patrolling security teams.

Human teams.

Theo lifted a shoulder toward Jared, who was silently waiting in the snow for the human duo to pass by the house. Immortals would be able to sense them, but apparently Saul felt safe enough with humans around. That was odd. There had only been four shifter guards near the house. Shouldn't there be more? Theo closed his eyes and tuned in to the world around him.

Nothing. Just the billowing wind and piercing cold.

He stilled and held up his hand for his brothers to stop. Why weren't there immortal signatures around? He moved closer to the white clapboard two-story. Shifters could mask their signatures, but there should still be some sort of hint. A blur of the atmosphere.

He was getting nothing.

The human guards finally passed, good-naturedly arguing about some movie.

Theo was just about to call his brothers over when he spotted movement inside the home. Ducking low, he moved to the window to see Saul Libscombe inside a rec room complete with wall-wide television, pool table, and dartboards. Last year's Superbowl was playing across the screen in vivid color.

The bastard had a glass of amber-colored whiskey in one hand and the remote control in the other. Apparently torturing Ginny earlier that day hadn't fazed him any. Oh, he was going to bleed.

Theo gave the hand signal, and his brothers disappeared around the corners.

He brushed snow from his eyes and angled back around toward the door. Chalton had already cut the feed for the alarm, so unless there were sensors Chalton hadn't found, which was pretty much impossible, Theo could walk right in. Taking a deep breath, he slid the wide door open and crossed into warmth, just as quietly closing the door.

The sound of the game in the other room was the only noise. He couldn't sense Saul, which was intriguing. The guy certainly had a way with electronics. Once Theo sliced him open, he'd have to search the place to see what all Saul had invented. After he turned off that damn ankle bracelet.

The ability to mask immortal signatures would be very much sought after. How had Saul done it?

Theo moved silently through the house, easily reaching the rec room just as Chalton and Jared entered from the other doors, their weapons already in their hands. Theo wanted to use his knife this time.

Saul turned. "Evening."

Theo stilled. Something wasn't right. He moved directly into the room. Holy fuck. The entire room was one massive screen. A modern-day hologram that looked fucking real from outside. "Retreat," he yelled, turning and rushing for the door. He'd almost reached the back when the ground rumbled and the air bunched.

The home exploded, throwing him high and far into the wild storm. Pain pierced through his skull. His last thought was of Ginny and her pretty blue eyes. Then blackness caught him before he hit the ground.

Chapter 10

Ginny stood outside the double protected bank vault. The Realm had gone with massive cast iron, concrete, and steel rods for reinforcement. It figured the king would use modern designs. Human designs, actually. Getting into the bank had been fairly easy, even though her command of the elements wasn't up to par.

Good thing she didn't need fire for this.

Oh, she still swirled around the oxygen and created a bit of ice, but that was much easier than fire to make. Apparently the king of the Realm wasn't too afraid of witches breaching his security.

He should know better.

The lock had a dual control mechanism with a time delay that was damn impressive. The biometric requirements were daunting as well. Of course, she'd helped to design this one as a side job more than a year ago.

One should never hire a thief to create security.

Humming softly, she drew out her key card and bypassed the design elements she'd installed. A backdoor was an absolute necessity, now wasn't it? The thrill of the hunt raced through her.

Could she truly give this up? Unlikely. Though she wouldn't steal from the king again. This was a one-time deal, and only because Saul had been torturing her for a decade. If he'd hurt her father, she'd destroy him. Three clicks echoed and then three more. The massive vault swung her way.

It was almost too easy.

She paused. It shouldn't be so easy. Wait a minute. She glanced up and then to the left. Aha. So the king had made a few adjustments. Nice laser and heat sensors. Good thing she was a witch. It would cost her, but she could reduce her heat signature to nothing. Drawing in air, she did so and then eyed the floor, which consisted of a series of square cement tiles. Interesting. A pattern.

Drawing out a device she'd invented nearly twenty years ago, she ran a laser with a gas medium over the floor. Two to the left, one right, two forward on the squares. She hopped, truly enjoying herself. Then she had to perform a cartwheel that made her almost giddy. Before she knew it, she was in front of Saul's safety deposit box. A wave of her hand, and any cameras went dark. Of course, when she waved, she blew high-pollinated PT dust, which she'd also invented. It would ruin the cameras for good.

She should probably figure out a way to send money anonymously to the Realm.

The actual box needed two keys. She withdrew the two masters from around her neck and inserted them, easily pulling out the drawer. One white envelope took up the entire thing.

She grasped it and shoved it into her back pocket before returning the drawer to rights. A quick glance around showed so many lovely boxes just waiting for her to explore. She sighed. No time. Maybe she could return if she didn't leave any evidence.

After retracing her steps from the vault and through the bank, she found herself outside in the wild snowstorm. Humming to herself, she turned to hustle back to Theo's place. The ductwork in his building was superior and had created an easy way in and out where she wouldn't be detected.

Lights flashed on outside the alley. An SUV started barreling toward her.

She paused, her body going still. Bloody Hell. Lights from above shone down, illuminating Saul in the passenger's seat. How the hell did he get free of Theo? Damn it. She turned to run, and pain licked up from her ankle. Crying out, she stumbled into the side of the building.

That asshole.

If he caught her, he could torture her until she gave up the location of the flash drive. Until she did that, he wouldn't kill her. So she ducked her head and ran, drawing on strength she hadn't known she possessed. Another prick to her ankle from the bracelet, and her leg went numb.

She fell into the snowy street, head first. Pain pummeled into her forehead.

"Hey." Three college-aged boys ran toward her. "Lady, you okay?" The first one, a tall dark-skinned kid wearing a letterman's jacket, gingerly lifted her up.

She sagged against him. "Sorry. Forgot my insulin earlier." That sounded okay, right?

The second kid, one wearing a similar jacket but with blond hair and a multitude of freckles, instantly grabbed a granola bar from his pocket. "Eat this."

She took it and forced a smile, glancing quickly around. The neighborhood held several bars with boisterous sounds emerging. A lot of young people strolled around in the snow, barhopping and being rather loud. She eyed the quiet SUV that had reached the end of the alley. Saul wouldn't want to cause a scene with so many security cameras around. She smiled at the young men, noting a stairwell down into the subway system. "I really need to head home, and I think that SUV is following me."

The boys instantly turned, their chests puffing out.

"We'll take care of it," the freckled kid said, starting to move.

"Thank you," she said, starting for the subway. If she could get on a car before she passed out, she might survive the night. "You're all kind, gentlemen." Oh, Saul wouldn't hurt humans with cameras around. But this was her only chance.

She barely made it down to the platform to buy a ticket and then limped onto the first train. Going to the back, she took a seat, having no idea where she'd end up. She pressed her head against the freezing window. Where was Theo? Was he all right? The fact that Saul had tracked her GPS to the bank wasn't good. Damn it. The GPS. She had to get back to safety before Saul tracked her.

Those boys wouldn't stop him for long.

She eyed the snowy darkness outside just as her vision began to fuzz from the planekite. Oh, this so wasn't good.

* * * *

Theo came to seconds after landing, his head ringing, snow up his nose. Groaning, he rolled over to see the entire house in flames. Fuck. He shoved to his feet, weaving, and tried to push through the snow. Chalton came barreling around the east side of the fire, burn marks across his head, his arm at an odd angle and blood flowing from his temple.

Relief caught Theo. "Jared?" he yelled.

Chalton looked frantically around, his clothes in tatters. Another explosion rocked the house, and he dropped to his knees. Theo ran forward and hauled him up, ignoring the pain as his broken ribs clattered together. He grunted and helped Chalton toward the other side of the house. Where the hell was Jared? Had he made it out of the house?

Sirens trilled in the distance, and people started coming out of homes to see the catastrophe. Fuck. They had to get out of there.

Theo tripped over a snow-laden bush, and Chalton stumbled, keeping them both going.

They found Jared free of the house, facedown in the snow. Flames licked across his vest, having burned through his jacket. Theo grabbed a handful of snow and slammed it down on the fire until the flames hissed into steam. "Jared?" He turned his brother over.

Jared's nose was broken along with what looked like his cheekbone. Blood flowed freely from a cut across his cheek. His breaths were shallow, but he was breathing and his heart seemed steady.

Theo shook him, but he didn't awaken. "We have to go." Grunting, he lifted his brother, and with Chalton's help, got him over Theo's shoulder. "Jesus. He weighs a ton." Staggering under the weight, bleeding, and with more bruises on his brain than he could count, Theo followed a limping Chalton through the backyard and toward the SUV they'd stashed down the private street.

They reached the vehicle, and Theo shoved Jared inside, following him into the backseat.

Chalton dodged around the front and ignited the engine, heading for the back exit to the subdivision. The sirens got louder, and the fire crackled merrily, even with the storm. "Fucking setup," Chalton muttered, swinging around a group of people in pajamas, boots, and heavy coats who were heading toward the fire. "How did he set us up?"

Theo shrugged, removing Jared's vest and lifting his shirt to see a myriad of bruises and obviously broken ribs. "Whoa." He patted Jared's hard cheek—the good one. "Wake up, bro."

Jared didn't move but tingles cascaded from him, so at least his system was repairing the damage. Good.

Theo shoved his tattered jacket off and gingerly felt along his own ribcage. Pain drew inward and spiraled out. Yep. Broken. He kept his eyes open but started sending healing cells first to his brain and then his body. "We need to figure this out."

"The trace on his call was good," Chalton said grimly, whipping the vehicle out onto a main road. "Saul did call for the car, but he must've realized we were ready to make a move. How? How could he possibly know we were working with Ginny and not against her?"

"She didn't tell him," Theo said wearily, leaning back.

"You sure?"

Theo studied his brother. "I'm sure." Even to get her father back, she wouldn't send Theo to his possible death. "I should tell you that we decided to mate. To save her life."

Chalton eyed him through the rearview mirror. "To save her life."

Jared snorted. "I'm half unconscious and even I know that's bullshit. To save her life. God, you're clueless."

Theo cut him a look. "Why don't you fix your face and not worry about me right now?"

Jared groaned and stronger tingles cascaded around him. "Veronica likes my face. I should heal it." He shifted on the seat. "You know what this means, right? The fact that we didn't find Saul?"

Theo nodded, grimness clutching his heart. "Yeah. Ginny has to go forward with the meet."

"If she hasn't already," Chalton said quietly.

"She hasn't," Theo snapped. "There's no way she turned us in to

Saul." The woman might be a thief and a manipulator, but she wouldn't purposefully cause harm. He just knew it.

"Say you're right and your future mate didn't call Saul and give him our information." Chalton sped up, moving quickly toward the city. "What if she didn't mean to tell him, but he still heard it from her?"

Theo rubbed his aching ribcage. "What do you mean?"

"What if—"

"Oh, shit." Theo smacked his head and then winced at the instant pain. "The anklet with GPS."

Chalton nodded, spraying snow and ice. "Yeah. It broadcasts location, but what if it also broadcasts sounds? What if he's been listening in the entire time?"

Theo's breath caught, and he fumbled for his phone, quickly dialing Ginny. "If he knows we left her…"

Chalton shook his head. "We left the place well guarded. If there had been any sort of problem, the guards would've called in."

Good point. But Theo's heart started beating faster as she didn't answer. "Ginny. Call me. Now." He left a message.

"She's probably asleep," Jared mumbled, keeping his eyes closed.

Theo looked at his brother. "Fix your face, would you?" That was true. Ginny could be asleep. But wouldn't she answer, considering he was on a mission to take out Saul? She would. He dialed the guards. "Check my apartment. Now."

"Affirmative," came across the line.

He held his breath. Heavy footsteps sounded, and then nothing. "Hello?" he said, his voice clipped.

The guard cleared his throat. "The apartment is empty. She didn't get by us, and there's no sign of a struggle."

"Secure the location," Theo said tersely, clicking off. "I'm going to fucking kill her."

Chapter 11

Ginny climbed through the vents before dawn, her hands freezing and her nose numb. After riding subway cars for hours and then maneuvering through the cold city, she'd finally arrived back at Theo's building. It wasn't dawn yet, so perhaps he hadn't made it home. She had to believe he'd lived through whatever Saul had planned for him.

Saul had almost caught her several times during the last few hours, but she was a master at getting in and out of tight spots.

The planekite had left her system, so she was feeling marginally better. Whatever she had in her pocket had kept Saul from killing her or even dosing her again, so she desperately needed to open that envelope.

But first, she had to get safely back into Theo's place.

Hopefully, he hadn't made it home yet.

She slid the vent in front of the kitchen open, dropped to the counter, and then back-flipped to the floor. Then she turned around and let out a small shriek.

Theo sat in a kitchen chair, bruises across his face, fury burning hot and bright in his dark eyes.

She clasped her hand to her chest and felt her thundering heart. "You scared the hell out of me."

He cocked his head slowly, the movement predatory. His dark shirt emphasized solid muscles, as did his faded jeans. Although his feet were bare, even they looked capable of great danger.

She swallowed, taking in his bruises. "I'm glad you're all right. I was worried."

He arched one dark eyebrow.

Okay. So he was a little angry. "I didn't know that Saul was setting you up," she said, trying to keep her voice calm.

Theo didn't move, but somehow more tension poured off him. "How do you know we were set up?"

She winced. "I may have seen him earlier tonight."

Both eyebrows arched.

"I, ah, saw him and ended up running all over the city trying to get back here," she said in a rush. Why couldn't she breathe? It wasn't like she was afraid of Theo. Not really. Sure, he looked like he could kill somebody right that moment, but why would he want to kill her?

"Are you all right?" Theo rumbled.

She nodded. "Yes. He engaged the anklet, but I got away. It was hours ago." Though she was starving all of a sudden. "What happened with you?"

"It was a trap that blew up. We're all fine," he said shortly, not losing any of his hard look.

She fought the very real urge to run out of the kitchen. By the look of him, she wouldn't make it. "I didn't promise to stay here."

Oops. He moved from the chair, walking for her fast, with a determined clip.

She backed up and hit the countertop. "What's—"

Then his hand was suddenly tangling in her hair and twisting. He moved her head to the side and pulled back until she faced him. Her brain just plain and simple stopped working. Vulnerability and an intriguing breathlessness caught her and held as tightly as he did.

He lowered his head until his eyes were right above hers. All of those interesting shades of black. As she watched, the sparkle turned to a deep metallic green. Stunning. His vampire colors. "I told you to stay here," he gritted out.

"I know." Wow. Those eyes were amazing. The myriad shades of both green and black was fascinating. "I, ah, am not really a sit around and wait type of lass." Her brogue emerged with her breathiness.

If anything, more anger poured from him. "In direct opposition to your sweet and helpless act."

She frowned. "Well, yes. I thought you knew that." Her brain was still fuzzy. He was too close. Lord, she still couldn't breathe.

His phone rang a bizarre tune that sounded somehow frantic. An emergency tune, without question. Without releasing her, he reached for it on the counter and pressed a button. "What?" he barked.

"Tell me Ginny didn't rob a Realm bank tonight," Chalton said urgently. "Please."

She blanched.

"Damn it," Theo muttered. "Give me the status."

"Dage called and has me tracking down who robbed the bank." Chalton's voice was both panicked and weary.

She barely kept back a smile. "He won't find me."

"Don't speak," Theo snarled, tightening his hold in her hair. "Not a fucking word."

Chalton sighed over the line. "I'll have her in about an hour. The surrounding buildings have devices I invented with heat, video, and even sound. The devices are compiling a recording right now of the person who broke into the bank, and she'll be recognizable by morning."

Her stomach dropped, even while her mind finally engaged. "I would love to see that technology. Fascinating. The surrounding buildings—what a remarkable idea."

Theo growled. A true, furious, masculine vampiric growl.

She shivered. Her nipples went hard as rocks. Even her knees weakened.

"How long can you hold off on telling the king?" Theo ground out, his breath warm on her face.

"As long as you need," Chalton said. "Want me to blow the evidence?"

Theo closed his eyes and quickly reopened them. "No. The king is almost a brother to you. I appreciate the offer, but do your job. Just do it slowly."

"Copy that. And good luck." Chalton clicked off.

She twisted her lip. "So. I may have broken into a Realm bank tonight." Would the king call for her head? She'd heard he was a reasonable guy, but he was still a vampire. "Is there a Realm prison somewhere?" She'd escaped a human prison back in the seventies, and it'd be nice to test those skills again.

"You're not going to prison," Theo said. "We'll figure something out. What did you find?"

She took out the envelope and ripped it open, dropping a flash drive in her hand. "To think we can now take each other down with these."

Theo grasped it and plugged it into a tablet on the counter, the tension still pouring from him. "It's encrypted. I'll set a program on it while we conclude matters." He typed on the small attached keyboard and then turned her way.

She wanted to back away again, but there was nowhere to go. "I can handle prison."

Theo shook his head. "I don't think the king would send his best friend's brother's mate to prison. Dage is all about family and connections."

Her mouth opened. "You still want to mate me?"

"Yes. Right now, actually." He didn't offer any other explanation, and the green in his eyes completely overtook the black. "You need it to survive, and I need it to have a hold on you. Forever." Then he kissed her. Holding her in place, he plundered deep.

Electricity jolted through her body. The kisses from him before... Those were different. Sweet and exploring. This was firm, deep, and hot. A claiming. Whatever she'd sensed in Theo, that predator he banked low with humor and watchfulness...was unleashed. He treated her like she was a strong woman. One who could take what he wanted to give.

That alone made her want to mate him. She was a gambler, and this would be the biggest gamble of her long life.

Then he gentled the kiss, starting to back her across the kitchen. Oh, hell no. If this was going to happen, and she wanted it to happen, he didn't get to treat her like the fragile thing she'd pretended to be for so long. She jerked her mouth free. "What are you doing?"

"Going to the bedroom." His hold lightened, even as his body was a long tense line of contained power. "I won't hurt you, Gin. You can trust me."

Ah, the sweet vampire. If she'd wanted to be coddled, she would've accepted one of the many offers to basically sit on a mated pedestal through the years. So she shot a punch into his gut, giving her just enough room to slip out of his grasp.

His chin lifted in warning, and those stark eyes glittered. "What are you doing?"

She edged around the counter and toward the door. "I don't want gentle or sweet. In fact, I don't want a wimp of a mate. I need pure strength and power."

Now his chin lowered. "You think I can't protect you?"

Sure, he could protect her when she needed it. But she wanted all of him—not just the protector. "I'm fairly capable, Theo." She moved backward, keeping him in her sights, into the living area. Pain flashed along her palm. Real pain, like a deep burn. Oh God. She glanced down. The marking. The Celtic knot, winding and beautiful, that presented itself when a witch found her mate. She couldn't breathe.

He stalked her, his steps slow and measured. "What game are you playing now?"

She swallowed, focusing back on him. This was really happening. "No game. I don't want a mate I can lead around by the nose. You want me?" she whispered, stepping toward the sofas.

"You know I do." He kept coming, his movement fluid. "Stop playing."

"Make me." With a quick move, she made it around the sofa, putting it between them. Her heart thundered, and her body had sprung fully alive. Pushing him was a bad idea, horrible, really, yet she knew what she wanted. Theo unleashed. "I used to watch you, T."

"Did you, now?" He stopped on the other side of the sofa, in complete control of the room. "And?"

"You're uncontrollable." The idea thrilled her to the point of being too dangerous. "That's why I didn't choose you back then."

At the reminder of her messing with his brother, he changed. Nothing obvious. She noticed it because she'd watched him secretly for years. She'd wanted him so badly for eons. His eyes glittered, focusing on her with a preternatural stillness. Here was the deadly soldier she'd heard whispered about from immortals who actually feared him.

The predator he hid down deep. Brutal, primal, and terrifying.

She wanted to make him hers. "Your calm façade is disappearing, Reese. You're looking a bit deadly," she breathed, her abdomen quivering.

"I am deadly. You might want to keep that in mind." His voice had lowered, turning gravelly hoarse.

The tone bit across her skin, heading down to the pulse between her legs.

He lifted his face, his nostrils flaring. "You're aroused, baby."

"That's impolite," she returned, moving slightly to the left.

"We left politeness a long time ago." He matched her movement. "I'm going to give you one more chance. Get your ass into the bedroom. Now."

"That's not what I want," she whispered, eyeing him, preparing to run. "Not even close. The question is: What do you want?"

"You." He was up and over the sofa in a wisp of sound.

She'd been waiting. She somersaulted in the air over the nearest chair, landing by the window. "You're fast."

"So are you." He stalked her around the chair, his hungry eyes unblinking and focused like any predator on prey. Her challenge had stripped him down to the dark and primitive beast at his core.

At that look, alarm trembled through her along with anticipation. She'd wanted him unleashed. Now could she handle him? The need to run was real this time. She feinted left and went right, rushing for the bedroom and the door that hopefully had a lock.

He caught her by the nape and the waistband, ripping her off her feet and flinging her over his shoulder. Not missing a beat, he strode toward the bedroom and kicked the door shut with enough strength to crack the door frame. One hand planted on her ass, and he flipped her over, tossing her on the bed.

Her shoulders hit first, and the wind whooshed out of her lungs. Before she could strike out, he'd ripped her jeans free of her body. She rolled to the side and tried to lever off the bed, a shocked laugh escaping her when he planted one hand across her entire lower back and somehow ripped off her shirt. She squirmed on the bed like a wriggling kitten, fighting to get free, wanting him to keep her close but unwilling to give in so easily.

She couldn't dislodge his hand.

He waited, the patient hunter, with her wearing nothing but her thin bra and panty set.

The bra released. "You ever been tied up?" he asked, no exertion in his voice.

"No," she gasped. A slow burn rolled through her body. He held her down with one hand, her face in the bedclothes, her feet kicking uselessly. The man had been bruised and burned. How was he fighting so well and easily? Adrenaline was flooding her body, giving her strength, but she couldn't match him.

Her thighs rubbed together, and she bit back a groan. "If I had my fire, I'd burn you to a crisp."

"This is for leaving the apartment." The smack to her ass shocked the heck out of her. She arched, gasping. Fire shot through her skin, followed by a chill that made her tremble.

He slapped her butt again, making her skin come alive with brutal tingles. "This is for robbing a bank. A Realm bank." Three very hard smacks followed in rapid succession.

She cried out and arched again, every nerve sparking. Nobody had dared treat her so, and yet she was primed and ready for him. Her breasts felt heavy and needy, while her sex contracted several times, needing something. Needing Theo Reese. She clenched her jaw to keep from begging for him.

He held his hand against her smarting rear, holding in the heat. She panted, her eyes wide, wondering what he'd do next. After the count of two heartbeats, he flipped her over.

Then he was on her.

Finally.

Chapter 12

Theo had waited too many damn long years to wait any longer. He kissed Ginny, and the taste of woman exploded on his tongue. Honey and spice and all intrigue. She tunneled her hands through his hair, kissing him back, her body softening for him. Her thighs rose on either side of his hips, and his jeans suddenly felt way too tight.

He leaned to the side, and she helped him tug his shirt over his head. Then he kicked his jeans to the ground. Wait. He had to make sure. "Ginny."

She grabbed his head and pulled him back down, her mouth seeking his.

"Wait," he said, grasping her hands and pressing them on either side of her head. "I have to know. You need to say it."

She blinked, her blue eyes dark pools of need. "Yes, Theo. To the mating. Not just to live, either. I want you."

He'd wanted her for centuries, and he'd never thought he'd hear those words from her. Not really. There were so many words and promises he wanted to give to her, but she widened her legs, and he could feel her heat. "You like being spanked."

Fire flashed in those eyes. "I most certainly do not."

That brogue in such a classy voice nearly made him come right then and there. He kissed her hard, forcing his body to relax as he brushed the bra off her arms. "You're lying to yourself if you believe that. Regardless, you should probably behave from now on," he said, his mouth against the pounding pulse in her neck.

"Not a chance," she breathed, arching into his body. Then she paused. "Wait a minute."

Hell, no. But he levered up, letting his bare chest rub against her hardened nipples. God, she was fucking amazing. "What?"

She writhed against him, somehow frowning. "I may be a fugitive. I don't want you in trouble with the Realm just because of me."

The woman was worried about him? His heart did a long roll, and his cock pulsed against her core. She was so warm and wet. "I won't let you go to jail, sweetheart."

Her light eyebrows arched. "Oh, I can get out of any jail. I was just worried you'd go to war or something."

Get out of jail? She looked intrigued…not frightened. His gaze narrowed. "You are not going to jail or breaking out of jail." It'd take a millennium to figure her out. Three of them to tame her. Good damn thing he was immortal. "Get that out of your head right now."

Her pout was cute and sexy at the same time. God, he wanted to bind her to him forever. He'd figure out why and what to do with her later. Right now, his fangs ached with the need to take a bite. He let them slide down.

Her eyes widened, and she stilled beneath him. "I've never been bitten before. By anybody." She swallowed.

"Get used to it." He scraped along her jugular, adding pressure but not harming her. Grinning, he licked across her neck and kissed her collarbone, heading down to her amazing breasts.

She hitched her breath.

He licked her, nipping and sucking, careful to keep his fangs from harming her. The threat was there, and she held still. He flicked a nipple, enjoying her startled gasp. "I've waited so long to touch you." To think he'd almost lost her. What if Saul had pressed the button? Theo kept kissing his way down her torso, wanting nothing more than to taste her again. He had to get the mating process going to protect her in case Saul did give her too much planekite. No matter what.

Her legs trembled when he reached her core, and he slid his

fangs in one inner thigh.

She cried out, the sound surprised and full of pleasure. "Shouldn't that hurt more?" she gasped, her nails raking the bedclothes.

He pulled them out, licking the wound closed. "They're too sharp for you to feel the pain." Unless he wanted to cause pain. That was a different matter. Then he licked along her slit, kissing her clit. He could spend all fucking year doing this. Licking her, making her squirm, listening to the sounds of pleasure she made.

His chest felt full, and the beast inside him, the one deep down, reared awake. Ready to possess and claim. But he needed her ready, because he was past being gentle. So he slid two fingers into her heat, twisting them, enjoying the arch of her against him. He sucked her clit into his mouth, not making her wait. She detonated, his name tumbling from her lips as she rode out the waves he tried to prolong.

Now that was sweet. His name from her. He'd waited a lifetime to hear that.

Maneuvering up, he kissed and licked, his body on fire for her. His cock throbbed like he'd been punched, and he needed to be inside her now.

He kissed her, and she ran her hands down his sides, pausing at the contusions still there. "Theo."

"Broken ribs," he confirmed. "House blew up."

She pushed his hair back, her eyes satisfied. "I'm so sorry. I wonder how he knew."

"Your anklet," Theo whispered right against her ear and then moved to pepper her jawline with kisses. "We think it broadcasts. He could hear us talking earlier." He kept his voice quiet enough that Saul couldn't hear.

"Oh." She kissed his forehead and then paused. Her body went wooden board stiff. "Wait a minute."

Fuck. He shouldn't have said anything.

She pushed him hard enough that he rolled off her, and then she bounded to stand. Her breasts bobbed, and panic filled her face. "He can *hear* us? Right now?" she mouthed silently, gesturing wildly.

Damn it. Theo stood, facing her down. "Yes," he mouthed just as silently. It didn't matter. This was going to happen, and right now, in order to protect her. It was the only way he could possibly keep her safe before the next mission. One they both had to go on. "Come here, Ginny."

* * * *

Oh, bloody to the hell and no. Ginny backed away, the offensive anklet feeling like it weighed a hundred pounds. Her body was flush with desire, even now, but this could *so* not happen. She held up a hand to ward off Theo.

Naked and fully aroused, he looked like an avenging god standing between her and the door. "Ginny."

The way he said her name—patience and determination and possession all rolled into two syllables. "No," she whispered, not willing to speak any louder, although if the damn thing could hear her, it probably could make out the slightest of sounds. God. She'd just orgasmed. *Loudly.*

As if reading her mind, Theo smiled, his fangs still showing. "You can scream my name as loud as you like for the world to hear," he mouthed, very clearly.

Heat flared into her face. She wanted to shush him, but he'd probably start talking louder so Saul could hear. Her clothes were on the floor, and she edged toward them.

"No," Theo said softly.

Why did that low voice send butterflies winging through her abdomen? The brand on her palm ached with the need to mark him, and her entire wrist was starting to hurt. She'd have to take the pain until she could get the anklet off. She pantomimed that they needed to get it off by pointing to it.

"After," he mouthed clearly.

She gulped.

"Ginny." He let his voice raise this time.

She panicked and waved her arms to shut him up. Saul wouldn't know what they were talking about. Well, he'd probably know, but he didn't know that they knew that he could hear. She shook her head. This was crazy.

Theo watched her, his gaze nearly physical. "Get back on the bed, Ginny."

Her sex clenched. Why in the thunder of the gods did that order, said in the gruff voice, turn her insides into lava? She went with her strengths and batted her eyes, fanning her face. "Theo? I need a moment. Please."

"No."

She coughed. No? He'd said *no*? She fanned harder, letting her body sway.

"Oh, knock it off. Get your ass on the bed or I'm going to put it there," he said, his gaze implacable.

She lost the act and glared. Why the hell couldn't she fool him? And now Saul knew full on that they were arguing about sex. She put her hands on her hips.

"That's better," Theo said, his chin lifting. His torso was wide and muscled, and his cock... Well, now. Hard, thick, and full. Apparently he had no problem standing there in the nude. Why would he? "Now, Ginny."

She only had one chance. Bunching her legs, she leaped for the door. He caught her around the waist, spinning her around and over the edge of the bed. She tried to stand, but he held her in place, her face to the bedspread, her feet on the plush carpet, her butt vulnerable to the vampire. Then he reached between her legs, his thumbnail scraping her clit.

Nerves fired, sending electricity through her. She was so primed and ready. Her body moved against him, shutting out her brain. He rubbed her, his talented fingers knowing just where to touch. How hard and how fast.

She bit her lip, pressing her mouth to the bed. No way would she make a sound. The hard slap of his other hand to her butt echoed through the room. Fire rushed through her, and she cried out. Another slap. This one she arched into. He lifted her all the way onto her hands and knees on the bed, his hand still working her, his body covering hers.

She rode his fingers, unable to stop. He kissed the back of her neck and reached around to pluck her nipples. Lord and saints, it was too much. He was everywhere, his mouth and fingers, his thighs and the hard press of his cock at her entrance.

He paused, and the world seemed to stop. "Ginny." It wasn't a question, but he still didn't move.

"Aye," she said, pushing back against him. Her body ruled. She wanted this, and she wanted him. All of him. "If you can catch me." She lunged forward.

He instantly banded an arm around her waist, yanking her back toward him. Then he gently guided himself inside her, his arm solid as steel, taking his time as he took her completely. Pain accompanied his movements, followed by a pleasure so intense she had to shut her eyes. He was so big, he filled everything she'd ever be.

Yet he went slow, letting her body get accustomed to him. Or maybe making sure she understood this was a claiming of the most primitive type. There was nothing she could do but accept him.

On his terms.

The fingers on her breasts tapped up until his hand settled on the front of her neck, holding firmly and lifting her head. She swallowed, her body open to him. Her heart flooded as he finally pushed all the way inside her.

Theo Reese. Completely inside her. Tears filled her eyes. *This.* This is what she'd waited for all these years. He touched every nerve she had, inside and outside, his body bracketing hers and holding her in place. He was all male, and she'd never, not ever, felt so much the female. Oh, she'd played. But she'd never felt this feminine. "Theo," she whispered.

"Yes." He pulled out and pushed back in, his movements slow and controlled. Then again. And again. Holding her in place, taking his time, taking her.

A quivering started deep inside her in a place she hadn't known existed. It spiraled out, circling.

She closed her eyes again just to feel, her body softening. The second she did, he increased the speed and depth of his thrusts, pulling her back each time so he could go deeper. He hammered into her, hard and fast, his breath turning ragged in her ear. The quivers turned to shakes and finally sparks of live electricity.

She broke first, screaming his name, the entire world exploding and then narrowing to right this second. His fangs flashed into her neck, going deep and striking bone. Pain detonated and then pleasure overwhelmed her, shooting throughout her entire body. She came hard, nearly sobbing with her orgasm.

His fangs retracted and he licked her shoulder before pulling out and rolling her onto her back. A second later, and he plunged inside her again, lifting one of her thighs to go deeper.

His eyes had turned a startling green. Crimson covered his high cheekbones, and his nostrils flared like a predator catching prey. He pounded inside her, his gaze intent.

She clasped her ankles around his big back and tilted her pelvis to take more of him.

He growled, and his fangs dropped again.

Instinctively, she turned her neck to grant him access. The second he slid the fangs back in, she planted her palm right over his heart. The marking flowed through her, from her core, and branded on his flesh with a heat that sparked white and fierce.

His fangs retracted, and he buried his head in her neck, shuddering as he came.

She gasped out air, her chest panting, and rubbed his back. Holy saints alive. She'd just mated Theo Reese. She could sleep for a year.

He lifted his head, a lock of hair falling across his forehead. "Now we get serious."

Chapter 13

Theo spent all day trying to decipher the damn flash drive, even inventing new computer programs on the spot. Chalton checked in on the phone several times, also working the problem from his place.

Ginny worked on her own laptop across the small table, blushing several times throughout the day.

Theo let her work through her feelings, finally settling back in his chair at the kitchen table, his gaze on her. She was squirming a little in her seat, and he bit back a grin. "Sore?"

She rolled her eyes. "No. By the way, what was up with the spanking?"

It was fun listening to modern slang in her old-fashioned brogue. "Don't put yourself in danger by robbing Realm banks, darlin'." Plus, she'd liked it.

She snorted. "This isn't a Lexi Blake novel, damn it. Keep your hands to yourself."

"You don't mean that," he said, letting the smile loose. They'd mated. They should probably talk about that, but it was more important they lived until the next day. He sobered. It was time to get serious. "The meet is tonight at midnight."

"I know," she said, glancing down at the ankle monitor, her jaw tightening.

Theo grabbed her phone off the counter, scrolled through the contacts, and dialed one. "Saul?" he asked, his voice a low rumble. "I've mated Ginny, which means you have no chance. Now tell me where to meet you, and I'll give you the flash drive in exchange for you removing the anklet and letting her father go." He pressed the speaker button and put the phone on the table.

She opened her mouth to argue, and Theo held up a hand. "Trust me," he mouthed. They couldn't let Saul know they'd figured out he could hear them.

Her frown didn't hold a hell of a lot of trust. More irritation, really.

"Theo, how lovely to hear your voice," Saul said, his tone even more nasally than before. "I have to say, I think Ginny could've done a lot better."

Ginny's face blazed a bright red.

Theo bit back irritation. "I think my mate is going to insist I gut you for that. Here I thought we'd reach an agreement like reasonable men." There was nothing reasonable about the way he was feeling. His hand itched to go for his knife. "Saul, where shall I meet you with the flash drive my mate stole from you yesterday?" Yeah. He'd said *my mate* twice.

"What flash drive?" Saul said. "Oh, the one planted in the Realm bank? There's nothing on it but a new encryption program I'm developing."

Theo arched an eyebrow at Ginny, who shrugged. "I'm not buying it. I bet I'll have it cracked by tonight," he said.

"Irrelevant," Saul said. "Here's the deal. I want Ginny and the Benjamin file at the meet. Not you. Not your brothers—assuming Jared survived last night. He wasn't moving after the explosion, now was he?"

The bastard had had cameras watching them. Theo forced a bored tone into his voice. "Dude, it's Jared. He's fine and now thirsting for your blood. You know. It's a normal Tuesday for him."

"If she's not alone, I kill her father," Saul said, his voice rising imperceptibly.

Theo moved to stop her from speaking, or to comfort her, but she stared at him calmly. Oh, sometimes even he forgot what a badass she could be. "It goes without saying, and yet I'm saying it anyway. If you hurt Elroy in any way, I'll hunt you to the end of my days. For sport." He tapped his fingers on the table. "Rumor has it I have a knack for hunting."

Saul audibly swallowed. "I want the file, Theo."

"Why?" Theo eyed the program running rapidly across his screen. "It's just family information. Some land ownings, other stocks, some secrets but nothing all that interesting."

"Oh, Theo." Saul chuckled, low and loud. "I know what's in there. The Green Rock file."

Fuck on motherfucker. Theo tensed but kept his voice level. "I have no clue what you're talking about." How had word gotten out, especially to a fucking shifter like Saul? Shit. Even if Theo somehow kept the file under wraps, he'd have to tell Chalton. Just so his brother had a heads-up. "You're inventing rumors."

"You know I'm not. I know about the file, and I want it. In addition to the rest of the information on Benny and the family. I'm actually surprised he hasn't come for your head yet," Saul said.

Oh, Benny was on his way, probably with his knife already sharpened. Or sword. Benny did love his swords. "Ben is family. That trumps everything." Theo shook his head at Ginny's inquisitive look. Benny would easily slice off Theo's head if given the opportunity. The guy really did see things in black and white, and sometimes family became too much of a pain in the ass for him.

"Tell Ginny I want her at midnight. I'm tired of dicking around here, Theo. Either she brings the flash drive or I'm letting the anklet finally do its job. Your mating is too new to protect her from the planekite, so I have to strike now before she can survive it. Tell the bitch she should've mated me." Saul clicked off.

"He is such a complete dick," Ginny said, glaring at the anklet.

Theo tensed for Saul to push whatever button he used, but nothing happened. Maybe the guy wanted Ginny at full strength for the night? Or maybe he didn't want to tip his hand that he could hear them. Sick asshole.

Theo's phone rang, and he glanced at it, seeing the queen's face on the screen. "Hello, Emma," he said by way of greeting, walking out of the room so Saul couldn't hear whatever was said. He gave Ginny a calm smile as he left, but she didn't look much reassured.

"Hello. Why is Saul Libscombe going through back channels to reach me about Virus-27?" Emma said, her voice short. "I asked

Dage, and he told me to give you a call."

Damn it. Theo's chest filled. "I assume Saul wants to try and negate the mating bond I just formed with Ginny O'Toole last night." The virus could negate a mating bond if one's mate was dead, but it hadn't been attempted in a living mate yet. So Saul still had plans for Ginny. Yeah. Theo was going to have to kill him. "Hey, how did Dage know about the mating?"

"He's the king," Emma said simply, her voice already distracted. "I'll make sure Saul doesn't get his hands on the virus. Say hi to Ginny for me." She ended the call.

Theo lifted his shirt to look at the perfect swirls of a Celtic knot right over his heart. Ginny had marked him but good. He smiled and turned to head back into the kitchen, where he arched an eyebrow. "You know the queen?"

A small smile played along Ginny's mouth. "I may have done a job or two for her through the years. Stealing proprietary information she could use in her work. Maybe."

Jesus. Sometimes the woman really caught him off guard. He grinned. Yeah, he liked that.

The front door opened, followed by footsteps as his brothers moved into the living room. Theo winked at Ginny and grabbed his laptop, motioning for her to stay in the kitchen. They had to keep Saul out of this plan. She blew a kiss at him as he left, warming his entire body.

He could feel the goofy smile on his face as he approached his brothers, but there was nothing he could do to stop it.

"Jesus. You mated. I can smell her on you." Jared clapped him on the back, a smile creasing his wide face. "Congrats."

"Thanks." Theo glanced at Chalton, who was grinning. "What?"

"Nothing. Just congrats." Chalton unpacked computer equipment and sat on the sofa. "I've figured out and have hacked into the anklet. The only way we can get it off her is to deactivate Saul's controller. Otherwise, the thing will explode and release enough planekite in her blood to kill her."

Theo sat on the leather chair and motioned for Jared to take the other one. "So, I didn't want to tell you this, but included in the Benjamin file is a series of data called the Green Rock file."

Jared groaned. "I thought we destroyed all of that information."

Chalton stiffened. "What's the Green Rock file?"

Theo searched for the right words. "Benny couldn't destroy the information because parties on the other side have it. It's a mutual opportunity for everyone to be protected from extortion and blackmail." He'd agreed with Benny. "But here's the deal. Ah, during the war, Benny might have, well he did, ah—"

"Jesus. What?" Chalton snapped, his angled face losing his normal calm expression.

"Benny collaborated with the demons. Before they became allies with the Realm. When they were, ah, killing vampires and kidnapping members of the Kayrs ruling family." Theo leaned back and waited for Chalton to lose his mind. He was close with the Kayrs family. Very.

Chalton paled. "Are you telling me that Benny helped facilitate the kidnapping of Jase Kayrs? My friend and the king's brother? The one who was tortured nearly to death and took forever to return to any normal life?" Chalton's voice darkened dangerously.

Maybe Theo should worry about Benny and not Chalton right now. "No. Benny had nothing to do with kidnapping Jase. But he did procure and deliver weapons to demon contacts during the war, some which may have been used against the Realm and to, ah, kidnap Jase."

"Damn it," Chalton said.

"We'll get the flash drive back," Theo said, determination filling his chest. "It can be our secret."

"Secrets get out." Chalton took his phone from his pocket and placed it on the coffee table next to the laptop.

Jared shook his head, his dark gaze on the phone like it might blow up. "Bro, I don't know Dage Kayrs like you do, considering you've worked with him for a century and I basically just met the guy. But I have heard all about him. Family is what he cares about. He'll kill all of us for even being associated with anybody who'd harmed his younger brother. Think about this."

Theo swallowed. "Agreed."

"I don't lie to my friends," Chalton said, watching his phone. "It's not who I am." He punched a couple of buttons on his phone and then turned toward the large flat screen over the fireplace, hacking it instantly to bring up a call to the king of the Realm.

Dage took shape, wearing a long black shirt with dark pants, his dark hair ruffled and his silver eyes curious. "Chalton? What's up?"

Chalton stood.

Theo faltered for a moment and then moved to stand next to his brother. Jared took point on the other side.

Dage lifted an eyebrow. "This is interesting."

Chalton nodded. "Not really. Information has come into my possession regarding my family's businesses, and more specifically, something called the Green Rock file."

"Oh, that." Dage waved a hand. "Benny and Ivan, you know the guy who owns Igor's, that bar downtown?"

Theo swallowed. "Yes. Ivan named the bar after his deceased brother."

"Yep. Benny and Ivan had a small business running weapons. Worked with the demons, the shifters, and sometimes even with us. I found out about it and gave Benny a deal he couldn't refuse." Dage's canines glinted. "He's a fun guy."

Chalton's shoulders visibly relaxed. "You knew about the Green Rock file?"

"Don't make me say it." Dage grinned. "The king, here. Besides, why didn't you just ask Ginny about the Green Rock file?"

Theo stilled. The blood rushed through his ears, ringing loudly. "Ginny?" he croaked.

Dage's forehead wrinkled, and delight darkened the silver in his eyes. "Oh. Well. Hmmm." He glanced to the side. "Coming," he called out loudly.

"Nobody just yelled for you," Theo countered. "Tell me—"

"Nope," the king said cheerfully. "My regards to your mate." The screen went black.

Theo lifted his head. "Ginny?" he bellowed.

Before she could respond, the front door crashed open, and a fully armed vampire dressed in combat gear stomped inside, fury on his face, his size eighteen boots cracking the tiles as he stomped.

Ah, shit. Theo sighed. "Hi, Uncle Benny."

"Goddamn it. Don't *uncle* me. I'm going to kill you

motherfuckers." Benny, his eyes a swirling mass of different metallic colors, lifted a green gun and pointed it at them.

Ginny moved in from the kitchen, and Theo leaped to cover her.

Her face brightened in a smile. "Benjamin!" Taking a leap, she rushed him, jumping for a hug.

The massive vampire dropped his gun and caught her, swinging her around. "Ginny, girl. You sweetheart. What are you doing here?" He seemed to forget all about Theo and his brothers.

Theo moved forward, his mind spinning and his chest heating. His woman had some serious explaining to do. "Put my mate down, Benny."

Benny gently set Ginny on her feet as if handling fine china, his face falling. "You mated him?"

She nodded, her dimple twinkling. "You disappointed?"

"Yes," Benny said, his body relaxing and his full lips turning down. "Now I probably can't kill him." He paused, his eyebrows lifting. "Right?"

Chapter 14

Ginny tried to plaster an innocent expression on her face, but from the glowering coming from her new mate, she wasn't successful. "I'd really appreciate it if we kept the killing to a minimum." Including her. Theo kind of looked like he wanted to strangle her. Or Benny. Or perhaps both of them. He did have two hands. "Please?"

Benny shuffled his humongous feet. "Oh, all right."

"Thank you." She gifted him with a genuine smile.

Benny was over a thousand years old. He had metallic eyes, long dark hair, a broad jaw, and a barrel of a chest. Standing at about six-foot-seven, he was a huge, sweet, deadly teddy bear, and she'd considered him one of her uncles for eons, even though he truly was shockingly handsome in a totally wounded and fallen angel way. "So you stole my file," he murmured, losing his smile.

"Aye," she said, sighing. "I'm sorry, but Saul has my da."

"Why didn't you call me?" Benny asked, hurt in his eyes.

She widened her eyes. "I tried. You've been in Russia, totally out of communication, Ben. I couldn't find you."

Now he blanched. "Ah, darling. I'm sorry. I needed a couple of decades of alone time." He turned a harsh glare on his nephews, seemingly uncaring that they were three of the most dangerous vampires in the world. "And you three jackasses got two of my places blown up. Destroyed. Completely turned to ash." His voice lowered to a growl that sounded more bear than wolf.

Theo stepped forward. "We've had a rough month, but we'll pay you back."

"Pay me back?" Benny boomed. "Oh, hell no. You'll overpay me until you work your fool fingers to the bone."

Theo's pupils narrowed as if his temper was stretching wide awake. "For fuck's sake, Ben. It was a penthouse and a house. Surely you had insurance." Theo looked like he'd be just fine if Benny punched him in the face. Oh, man. Theo wanted a good fight and right now. "Would you just get over it?" He tensed, apparently ready for the blow.

Benny looked at him. Then at Ginny. Then once again at Theo. A smile twitched on his lips. Then he threw back his head and laughed, the boisterous sound echoing in every direction. His eyes watered, and he wiped them off, finally sobering with a couple of coughs. "Oh, boy. You just have no clue what you've gotten into."

Theo cut a hard look toward Ginny. "I'm getting the idea that may be true."

She fought the very real urge to stick her tongue out at him. Sometimes a vampire ended up pushed to his limit, and if she had to guess, Theo had reached that point more than a few hours earlier. "I've never pretended to be anything but who I am."

Theo snorted. "Are you fucking kidding me?"

Heat filled her face. "All right. I haven't pretended since I promised you I wouldn't." All saints. What did he want, anyway?

Theo turned suddenly more toward Benny. "Why the hell didn't you tell me the king knew about the Green Rock file?"

Benny's broad forehead wrinkled. "Huh. Thought I had. Why do you care, anyway?"

Red flushed across Theo's handsome face, even reaching his ears.

Ginny stepped in, patting Theo's wide chest. "Um, I think perhaps Theo was concerned that the king would be angry. Considering Chalton works with the Realm, surely you can understand that concern, Benny." She smiled at him again as if he should most certainly understand.

He stared at her a moment. "Well, uh, yeah. I guess I do understand that now." He cleared his throat and looked at Theo. "I, ah, I'm sorry I didn't tell you about that." His brows drew down and he looked at Ginny for confirmation. When she nodded with encouragement, his face cleared. "Yeah. Shoulda told you."

Theo looked down at her as if the world had started spinning backward all of a sudden. "Have you two, ah, worked together a lot?"

Benny chuckled. "Oh, yeah. Remember that cadre of wolf shifters we—"

Ginny held up a hand. "Oh, my." Panic cut through her with a large swath. Theo didn't need to know about some of the scrapes she, Benny, and her father had gotten into through the years. "We don't want to bother Theo with *that* story." Glancing to the side, she caught both of Theo's brothers staring at her, their mouths open and their brows furrowed. Amusement glittered in Jared's eyes, while Chalton just looked bemused.

Theo looked like he'd been hit in the head with a concrete block. Twice. "Cadre of wolves?"

"Wasn't nearly as interesting as when we infiltrated the dragon island. When was that? About thirty years ago?" Benny rubbed his broad jaw, his lips quirking.

Oh, man. Benny couldn't catch a hint. She pressed her lips together and shook her head at him.

"You don't remember the dragons?" Benny asked, his brow furrowing.

Theo swallowed. "We've just recently discovered that there are dragons and that they live on an invisible island. You two, ah, knew three decades ago that dragons existed?" He looked almost dazed.

Benny laughed again, his rock-hard belly visibly clenching beneath his black shirt. "Obviously. How else would we have stolen the rubies?"

"Rubies." Theo wavered. "You stole rubies from *dragons*."

"To be fair, they stole them first," Ginny rushed to say. This was going south and way too quickly. "So, Benny. In town for long?"

Benny chewed on his lip. "Nope. Just came to get my flash drive back."

She cleared her throat, her stomach churning. "I can't give it to you, Ben. I'm so sorry. But I made a deal with Saul."

Benny sighed loudly. Very loudly. "I understand. A deal's a deal." He spread his arms out and looked at the three Reese men.

"Well? I can't torture her for information. We've been friends for too long. Which one of you is up to the task?"

"Nobody is torturing my mate." Theo tucked her close into his side. His computer dinged, and he glanced over at it.

Ginny partially turned, not even remotely worried that any of the four males would try to torture her. Please. Theo had to see through his uncle. Benny wouldn't hurt a woman. Code flashed across the screen. Her breath caught. Theo had cracked the code on Saul's flash drive.

Good. Now they could finally find something to trade. She moved for it.

Theo held her still. "While nobody is going to torture my mate, I am going to get the information from her." He pointed toward the laptop, and Chalton nodded, hustling toward it. "Excuse us," Theo said, drawing her toward the bedroom.

"There you go, Theo," Benny said agreeably. "I'll make some sandwiches while you get the info from her. You'd better have roast beef." He started moving toward the kitchen. "Boys, start plying me with plans to repay me for your destructive last month. I came here to slice off somebody's head, and I'm not thrilled I don't get to play today."

Theo tugged her toward the bedroom.

She stumbled, looking back at the computer. Was he serious? "I'm not going to tell you," she said, figuring it was only fair to warn him.

"The hell you're not," he said grimly, drawing her inside and shutting the door. Hard.

* * * *

Ginny stumbled and then drew free, backing toward the bed. Ice pricked down her back. "Listen, Theo."

"No. You listen." He leaned against the door, his arms crossed. His brown hair was mussed, and a fine shadow covered his angled jaw. He looked big and broad and unbeatable. "I'm finished with this bullshit. Tell me where the flash drive is, and I'll take it to Saul to get your father back."

Just looking at him made her mouth water. Why was he saying these things? "I can't. He's serious." Her voice trembled. Theo seemed to have lost his mind.

"I'm serious." He looked implacable, as impenetrable as rock. "I'll trade what you stole for the flash drive. But I'm done negotiating with you." Moving for her, he manacled her hair, bringing her up on her toes.

She gasped, panic and anger coursing through her. "Theo, you're hurting me."

He blinked and loosened his hold, his voice remaining cold and rough. "I'll hurt you a lot more if you don't give in." Gently, he rubbed her head. Then he winked.

What? Oh. Of course. This was for Saul's benefit.

She lowered her chin. Well, then. She sniffed and let the tears fall. "Oh, Theo, I just..." She coughed several times, giving it all she had. "I'm so tired and sore. Last night we mated, and I—" Her voice rose in one of her best performances. "I'm just not strong like you."

He rolled his eyes and drew her close. "Oh, Ginny. I'm so sorry. For a moment, with all the stories, I forgot how delicate you are." Leaning back, he shook his head, his lip quirking. "You should be protected and cosseted, and that's my job now." His eyes rolled so far back, it was a wonder he couldn't see his brain.

She grinned but forced a couple of hiccups. "I, I just need rest. Just an hour, please? We can talk after that."

"Okay. I'll go eat with my brothers." He kissed her loudly on the cheek. "Just rest, babykins."

Babykins? Seriously? Talk about overplaying the role. The vampire sucked at acting. She shook her head and shoved him in the gut. "Thank you so much, Theo. I do trust you to protect me." Her voice went breathy and weak.

"Jesus," he mouthed. "Stay here. I'll be back with a plan." Turning her, he smacked her ass. She whirled back around, but he was already out the door.

She sat down, kicking her heels. After about five minutes, she started creating escape plans from the room. Those vents were truly a gift for somebody like her. Keeping as quiet as she could, trying to make Saul think she was taking a nap or crying or something, she lifted the bedside table toward the door and the vent.

Theo walked in. He took one look at her and spread his arms out in a "what the hell?" movement.

She bit back a grin and pointed to the vents and obvious escape route.

He sighed, shaking his head. Then he handed over a piece of paper.

SAUL'S FLASH DRIVE HELD PLANS TO INFILTRATE REALM HEADQUARTERS AND TAKE BRENNA DUNNE-KAYRS. SHE'S A WITCH, AND HE PLANNED TO PUT AN ANKLET ON HER. SINCE SHE'S ON THE RULING BODY OF WITCHES, HE HAD BIG PLANS TO TAKE OVER. THE WITCHES ARE IN FLUX RIGHT NOW, AS YOU KNOW.

Ginny read, her mind spinning. Wasn't Brenna pregnant? What would an anklet like that do to a pregnant witch? Ginny's stomach rolled, and bile rose in her throat. She swallowed rapidly.

Theo handed her another piece of paper, and she read, trying not to crinkle it or make any noise.

THE PLAN TONIGHT AT MIDNIGHT:

YOU AND I GET THE BENJAMIN FILE

WE TAKE IT AND THE FLASH DRIVE YOU STOLE TO THE MEET WITH SAUL. WE'LL PRETEND WE COULDN'T GET INTO HIS DOCUMENTS.

Ginny read the last line and shook her head, pointing at the script. Saul wouldn't believe them. He couldn't afford to. Theo calmly pointed at the next paragraph.

SAUL CAN'T AFFORD TO BELIEVE US. SO WE MOVE IN AND TAKE HIM, FORCING HIM TO GIVE UP THE CONTROLLER FOR THE ANKLET.

Ginny sighed. It was a nice plan and she hated to disagree. But it wouldn't work. She motioned for a pen, and Theo handed one over, and she started to write:

THE MEET IS SET FOR OUTSIDE MARIO PIZZA'S BACK ENTRANCE. A CAR IS PICKING ME UP. I DON'T ACTUALLY KNOW WHERE THE MEET IS. I HAVE TO GO ALONE, BUT YOU CAN PUT A TRACKER ON ME. IT'S THE ONLY WAY.

It truly was the only way. Saul wouldn't let his guard down if she had a vampire soldier with her. He'd already proven he was smarter than she'd feared.

She started writing again:

YOU'RE GOING TO HAVE TO TRUST ME THIS TIME.

Theo studied her, his eyes veiled. "I'll be back in a few," he mouthed, turning and shutting the door so he could probably speak with his brothers without being overheard by Saul.

She waited two minutes, looking at the closed door. Everything she'd ever wanted was on the other side, but she had to save her father. The flash drive she'd stolen had been cracked, and Saul would assume it had, so there really was no reason for her to return it. What he wanted she had stashed across town.

Glancing at the bed that had changed her life, she stood on the table and opened the vent. There was only one path to take here. God, she hoped Theo forgave her.

If she lived.

Chapter 15

A town car pulled up next to Ginny outside the pizza restaurant at exactly midnight. She opened the door and slid inside, grateful to be out of the snow. They drove through town, and the merry Christmas lights and decorations covered most surfaces in sparkle and spirit. She swallowed, her mind on Theo.

There had been so many things she'd wanted to say to him, but there hadn't been time. And a stupid anklet broadcast her every sound. She really tried not to think about that.

The partition was up between her and the driver, so she settled back in the seat and watched the Christmas lights fly by. The car smelled like new leather.

They finally pulled up in front of a closed jewelry store. She stepped outside, noting the door was open. Glancing around, she couldn't see anybody on the street. Was this some sort of odd trap? Steeling her shoulders, she moved gingerly through the heavy snow and strode inside the shop.

The lights came on, and the door shut behind her. "Saul," she murmured.

Saul Libscombe sat across the room and behind a low counter of what looked like opals. "I commend you for coming alone."

"You didn't give me a choice." She jumped when a man stepped out from the shadows behind her, slapping him when he tried to frisk her. "I'm not stupid enough to bring either flash drive." The goon gave up, and after Saul nodded, he walked around the counter and went through a door to the back room.

Saul stood about six feet tall, with light brown hair and stark blue eyes. He was fit and strong at about five centuries old, and he dressed like he enjoyed luxury in designer pants and a perfectly pressed silk shirt. His watch was a Rolex that wouldn't be released to humans for at least a year. "Where's the Benjamin file?" he asked, his gaze sharp.

"Where's my father?" she returned, holding her ground. There were counters of jewels all around her, but all she wanted was her da.

Saul let out a low whistle, and the goon from earlier shoved out her father.

"Da!" she cried out, rushing for him.

He enfolded her in a huge hug, smelling like peppermint and bourbon. His normal smell. "Ah, my girl. How I've missed you."

She leaned back. At nine centuries old, Elroy O'Toole was one handsome man. Blue eyes, blond hair, and sharp features. Like her. She checked him over, noting a scarf over his neck. Oh God. She grabbed for it, revealing a planekite collar. No wonder he hadn't been able to escape. She'd thought about it, but she hadn't wanted to really consider the possibility. "Oh, Da."

He hugged her again. "Hasn't been so bad. Only a decade, really. I've been worried about you." He smoothed back her hair.

She forced a smile. "I've been fine."

He paused, studying her. "Something's different." His eyes widened. "Oh, my."

"Aye," she murmured, knowing he could sense the mating. "You always did like Theo, remember?"

Her da slowly nodded. "'Tis true. I did."

That was good, at least. "Where have you been? I've looked everywhere."

"Moving around quite a bit," her da said wearily. "Ready to get this collar off."

Saul lifted a remote control in his hand. "Last chance, Ginny. Give me the location of the Benjamin file or I press the button. You both die."

She turned to face him, wanting nothing more than to be able to throw fire again. Wait a minute. She'd mated. Truth be told, she did feel stronger. A little. There was only one chance, but she'd take it. "I have it." Stepping away from her father, she made her way toward Saul. "The second you release these collars, I'll hand it over."

"No," Saul said. "Collars stay on, but I won't kill you. That's a good bargain. Take it."

She stood a foot away from him. The room had an odd lemon minty smell. Probably something Christmas related. "You've kept me enslaved for a decade. Do you really think you'll ever be safe from me?"

He smiled, revealing a crooked front tooth as he lifted the controller. "Aye. I truly do."

She drew deep, going for power, thinking of Theo. His strength, his humor, his passion. That lived in her now. She only needed a little. Just a little. "All right." Her shoulders slumping, she batted her eyelashes and looked fragile. Beaten. Weak.

Saul lowered his hand.

She shuddered hard and reached inside her coat. Theo. Power. Love. "I can throw fire now." Power flushed through her on the thought, and she drew out her hand, throwing her hand toward him.

Nothing happened, but the bluff worked. He yelped and jumped out of the way, not realizing there was no fire until he was already in motion. In one smooth movement, she planted her hands on the counter and flipped over, catching the controller with her ankles. Then she swung around, hit the ground, and kept rolling, coming up in front of her dad.

Saul bellowed and quickly lifted a green gun to point at her. The kind that shot lasers that turned to lead in immortals. Shit.

Her dad held out his hands. "Enough, Saul. Enough."

Saul fired, and the impact hit Elroy in the chest, throwing him back into the wall. He pushed Ginny out of the way as he fell. She glanced frantically at the controller. It had three green buttons. What the hell?

Saul laughed and moved toward her.

Her father struggled to a seated position, blood pouring from a wound near his neck.

"Heal that," she hissed. Oh, she was going to fight. She lifted her hand and nothing happened. Fire sputtered for just a second. Wow.

But that was it. No more fire. Damn it. That was all she had for the moment. She backed away, holding the controller. Saul came nearer, and she leaped up, kicking him beneath the chin. His jaw cracked. He stumbled back, his arms windmilling, fury in his holler.

His chin lowered. He turned and pointed the gun at her.

The front window crashed in, two bodies dropped from the ceiling, and the goon from before crashed through from the back, smashing into one of the counters and sending glass flying through the room.

And then all hell broke loose.

* * * *

Theo zeroed in on the threat to his mate immediately as he sprang through the glass window and kept going, straight into Saul Libscombe. Lasers impacted Theo's vest and pummeled his still healing ribs, but he didn't care. His knife was out, and he slashed across Saul's arms until the shifter dropped the gun.

Then he punched the bastard in the face. Once, twice, and then enough times he lost count.

Saul fought back, kicking and changing his nails into claws to rip into Theo's flesh.

Three shifter soldiers poured in from the back, and Theo caught Jared, Chalton, and Benny engaging in battles involving guns, knives, and some serious fang slashing.

Saul kept slashing at Theo, even while he took hit after hit after hit.

Theo didn't feel a thing. A raw possessiveness overtook him, destroying his ability to think rationally. He didn't give a shit. Ginny had been in danger, and now that threat was bleeding all over Theo. His neck was bleeding from deep gouges, and he kept swinging, carving pieces until Saul was one open wound.

A body flew over Theo's head, and he ducked after making sure it wasn't one of his team. Nope. Saul sliced a claw beneath his chin, and Theo bellowed. He saw red.

Shoving the shifter down onto his back on the floor, Theo followed him, straddling the bastard and punching all the way through to the cement. Bones shattered. More bloody claws, more temper. Damn it. Theo struck hard beneath the jaw and could hear Saul's skull crack.

Finally, the shifter stopped moving.

Theo panted, straddling the enemy, waiting for him to strike. Nothing.

"He's out, dude," Jared said, leaning down, his upper lip split wide open. "Totally."

Chalton wiped glass off his shirt, leaving a trail of blood from his bleeding knuckles. "You could kill him, but I think the Realm would really like to discuss his future kidnapping plans first. After going through the plans, it doesn't appear he was working alone. He has allies."

It was no fun to kill a guy he'd knocked out, anyway. Theo shoved to his feet, immediately turning. Shifter soldiers were unconscious in the corner, Benny was talking to Elroy O'Toole, who was already healing the bullet holes along his upper chest.

Ginny was watching him, her eyes wide, her face pale, and a black box held tightly in her hand.

Theo moved toward her. "You okay?"

"I kind of made fire," she said slowly, peering around him at Saul's body beaten to a bloody pulp. "He's gonna feel that for a long time."

"Good." Theo gingerly took the box from her. "Chalton?"

Chalton hustled over, yanking a tablet from his back pocket. "Yeah. Give me a sec." He started pushing buttons.

Theo brushed Ginny's hair away from her face, his heart finally settling. "You scared the hell out of me."

"I'm sorry." She leaned into his touch, her eyes darkening. "There wasn't a choice."

"I know." He pressed a soft kiss to her nose.

"You did?" She stiffened and then leaned back, studying him. "Wait a minute. How are you here right now?"

He was still too keyed up and pissed to grin, but it was nice catching her off balance for once. "Remember we hacked into the anklet? We followed you, lady. The entire time."

Her eyes lit up. "You knew I'd leave?"

"Yeah." He knew. It had been the hardest thing he'd ever done to let her go, but she'd been right. It had been the only good plan. And he'd covered her as soon as he could, although it had nearly eaten him up throughout. He'd discovered, right there and then, where his heart belonged. "I love you. Should've told you before. I've loved you for centuries."

She gasped, delight brushing even more beauty across her face. "I love you, too. Ever since we were kids so many years ago. It has always been you—only you."

He kissed her, going deep. A trio of clearing voices caught him, and he reluctantly released her mouth. For now. "Chalton?"

Chalton handed over the tablet. "Here's the frequency. You were right. It's the same one we hacked. Simple but efficient."

Theo took the tablet, read the code, and then quickly started typing. Then he hit ENTER.

Ginny gasped and kicked out her leg. The anklet went flying across the room to hit a counter and fall hard.

She breathed out several times.

Saul groaned and tried to roll over.

"Hell no." She stomped over and kicked him with the foot that had had to balance that anklet for so long. Then she kicked him again in the ribs. Hard. Then again.

"Should we stop her?" Chalton asked mildly.

Theo shrugged. "No. Let her play."

She kicked Saul in the temple, and the shifter fell into unconsciousness again. Her chest heaving, Ginny looked up and grinned.

God, she was beautiful.

Then she slowly looked around at all the jewelry on the ground.

"No," Theo said automatically.

She bit her lip. "Well? Who owns this place?"

"Saul does," Benny said quietly. "Always has."

Ginny did something that looked like a cross between a happy hop and a charge for the nearest emeralds lying all over the demolished floor. "If Saul owns these, they're coming home with me." Then she looked up, delight in her eyes. "Right, Theo?"

He couldn't help it. The woman was definitely a thief because she'd stolen his heart and it had taken him this long to realize it. If she wanted to steal, especially from a jerk who'd hurt her, Theo would make it happen. "Right, sweetheart. Let me find you a big bag."

Yeah. This was definitely love. The forever kind.

Epilogue

Helen Reese kicked her feet atop the coffee table and sipped on heavily laced eggnog in her comfortable living room. The lights on the tree twinkled in tune with the festive music from the hidden speakers. Contentment filled her along with the warmth. Her three boys were mated and in love, all gathered around the Christmas tree with strong and modern women.

"You did good." Benny sat next to her on the couch after having spiked the eggnog, his gaze on the younger generation. He flattened his boots on the coffee table, loudly breaking it in two.

She sighed and let her feet fall to the floor as the coffee table did the same. "Benjamin," she murmured. Centuries ago, she'd mated his brother, and Benny had become *her* brother. Even now that she'd been widowed for so long, she loved him as a brother. A pain-in-the-behind brother, but family nonetheless.

He snorted, his boots smashing the fallen magazines. "Sorry."

She shrugged. "It's just furniture." Then she smiled. "I did do good." Sure, she'd committed treason and possibly espionage when she'd maneuvered Chalton and Olivia together, but just look how happy they were.

Chalton leaned against the wall, his legs extended, his arm around his pretty Olivia. She rested against him, so much smaller than the vampire. She talked animatedly with Ronnie, who sat on Jared's lap on the settee, idly playing with his dark hair. Even after all these years, Jared still looked like a pirate. Helen grinned at her eldest son.

Benny patted his flat belly. "Yep. A journalist, a police psychologist, and a thief. All good mates for the boys."

"Yes," Helen murmured. She'd done it. Now that Theo had mated Ginny, they were all happily mated and would hopefully soon give her grandchildren. "You're next, Ben."

He snorted and drank his eggnog in one gulp. "Nope. Not me."

Helen turned toward him. He was huge, even for a vampire soldier. Solid barrel of a chest, long legs, dangerous hands. With his black hair and greenish-black eyes, he looked like a compilation of her sons. But bigger. "Why haven't you ever mated?"

He lifted a shoulder the size of a small mountain. "Why would I?"

Hmm. Maybe she'd just found her next project.

"Don't even think it." A small smile played on his lips as he watched his nephews. "Glad I didn't have to cut off anybody's head. It's a good holiday."

She rolled her eyes. Benny was a big talker, but he'd die for family. "It was kind of you to spare them." She could play along as his Christmas gift.

He nodded sagely. "Aye. It was." His sigh reminded her of a slumbering bear in the sun.

Ginny laughed at something Ronnie said, the sound tinkly and fun. She cuddled with Theo in the ottoman, pretty much lying in his lap.

Helen smiled. "They're happy." That made her happy.

"Good." Benny reached over his head for the pitcher on the sofa table and refilled their glasses. "Because peace ain't gonna last. Something's coming."

"I know," she said softly, as always attuned to the winds. "But not yet."

Benny shook his head. "Disagree, sister. The atmosphere is heavy. With change."

She sighed and watched him from the corner of her eye. Benny was older than even she knew, and he had a sense of the world she'd never understood. "What do you know?"

"Nothing. Yet." His solid block of a face remained calm, but a thread of caution rode his words.

"Benny," she said softly, to remind him they went way back. So many people thought Benny was crazy or just a big brute. But she knew him. There was more to Benjamin Reese than most people could see, and he enjoyed it like that. "Tell me."

"Helen, if I knew, I'd tell you." He set his glass down. "Whatever is coming will make an appearance soon enough."

She ignored the chill dancing down her back. Destiny always seemed cold. "What now?"

"Now?" He grinned and raised his voice. "Now my nephews are going to ply me with presents for being so damn fucking understanding when they blew up not one but two of my very nice homes."

The three boys groaned, already reaching for a myriad of wrapped presents.

"There had better be a pony in there," Benny rumbled.

Helen couldn't help but chuckle. For now.

Keep an eye out for more Dark Protector books in 2018. We're going back to the originals. (
XO
Rebecca

* * * *

Also from 1001 Dark Nights and Rebecca Zanetti, discover Teased and Tricked.

Sign up for the 1001 Dark Nights Newsletter
and be entered to win a Tiffany Key necklace.

There's a contest every month!

Go to www.1001DarkNights.com to subscribe.

As a bonus, all subscribers will receive a free
1001 Dark Nights story
The First Night
by Lexi Blake & M.J. Rose

Turn the page for a full list of the
1001 Dark Nights fabulous novellas...

Discover 1001 Dark Nights Collection Four

Go to www.1001DarkNights.com for more information.

ROCK CHICK REAWAKENING by Kristen Ashley
A Rock Chick Novella

ADORING INK by Carrie Ann Ryan
A Montgomery Ink Novella

SWEET RIVALRY by K. Bromberg

SHADE'S LADY by Joanna Wylde
A Reapers MC Novella

RAZR by Larissa Ione
A Demonica Underworld Novella

ARRANGED by Lexi Blake
A Masters and Mercenaries Novella

TANGLED by Rebecca Zanetti
A Dark Protectors Novella

HOLD ME by J. Kenner
A Stark Ever After Novella

SOMEHOW, SOME WAY by Jennifer Probst
A Billionaire Builders Novella

TOO CLOSE TO CALL by Tessa Bailey
A Romancing the Clarksons Novella

HUNTED by Elisabeth Naughton
An Eternal Guardians Novella

EYES ON YOU by Laura Kaye
A Blasphemy Novella

BLADE by Alexandra Ivy/Laura Wright
A Bayou Heat Novella

DRAGON BURN by Donna Grant
A Dark Kings Novella

TRIPPED OUT by Lorelei James
A Blacktop Cowboys® Novella

STUD FINDER by Lauren Blakely

MIDNIGHT UNLEASHED by Lara Adrian
A Midnight Breed Novella

HALLOW BE THE HAUNT by Heather Graham
A Krewe of Hunters Novella

DIRTY FILTHY FIX by Laurelin Paige
A Fixed Novella

THE BED MATE by Kendall Ryan
A Room Mate Novella

NIGHT GAMES by CD Reiss
A Games Novella

NO RESERVATIONS by Kristen Proby
A Fusion Novella

DAWN OF SURRENDER by Liliana Hart
A MacKenzie Family Novella

Discover 1001 Dark Nights Collection One

Go to www.1001DarkNights.com for more information.

FOREVER WICKED by Shayla Black
CRIMSON TWILIGHT by Heather Graham
CAPTURED IN SURRENDER by Liliana Hart
SILENT BITE: A SCANGUARDS WEDDING by Tina Folsom
DUNGEON GAMES by Lexi Blake
AZAGOTH by Larissa Ione
NEED YOU NOW by Lisa Renee Jones
SHOW ME, BABY by Cherise Sinclair
ROPED IN by Lorelei James
TEMPTED BY MIDNIGHT by Lara Adrian
THE FLAME by Christopher Rice
CARESS OF DARKNESS by Julie Kenner

Also from 1001 Dark Nights

TAME ME by J. Kenner

Discover 1001 Dark Nights Collection Two

Go to www.1001DarkNights.com for more information.

WICKED WOLF by Carrie Ann Ryan
WHEN IRISH EYES ARE HAUNTING by Heather Graham
EASY WITH YOU by Kristen Proby
MASTER OF FREEDOM by Cherise Sinclair
CARESS OF PLEASURE by Julie Kenner
ADORED by Lexi Blake
HADES by Larissa Ione
RAVAGED by Elisabeth Naughton
DREAM OF YOU by Jennifer L. Armentrout
STRIPPED DOWN by Lorelei James
RAGE/KILLIAN by Alexandra Ivy/Laura Wright
DRAGON KING by Donna Grant
PURE WICKED by Shayla Black
HARD AS STEEL by Laura Kaye
STROKE OF MIDNIGHT by Lara Adrian
ALL HALLOWS EVE by Heather Graham
KISS THE FLAME by Christopher Rice
DARING HER LOVE by Melissa Foster
TEASED by Rebecca Zanetti
THE PROMISE OF SURRENDER by Liliana Hart

Also from 1001 Dark Nights

THE SURRENDER GATE By Christopher Rice
SERVICING THE TARGET By Cherise Sinclair

Discover 1001 Dark Nights Collection Three

Go to www.1001DarkNights.com for more information.

HIDDEN INK by Carrie Ann Ryan
BLOOD ON THE BAYOU by Heather Graham
SEARCHING FOR MINE by Jennifer Probst
DANCE OF DESIRE by Christopher Rice
ROUGH RHYTHM by Tessa Bailey
DEVOTED by Lexi Blake
Z by Larissa Ione
FALLING UNDER YOU by Laurelin Paige
EASY FOR KEEPS by Kristen Proby
UNCHAINED by Elisabeth Naughton
HARD TO SERVE by Laura Kaye
DRAGON FEVER by Donna Grant
KAYDEN/SIMON by Alexandra Ivy/Laura Wright
STRUNG UP by Lorelei James
MIDNIGHT UNTAMED by Lara Adrian
TRICKED by Rebecca Zanetti
DIRTY WICKED by Shayla Black
THE ONLY ONE by Lauren Blakely
SWEET SURRENDER by Liliana Hart

About Rebecca Zanetti

Rebecca Zanetti is the author of over thirty romantic suspense and dark paranormal novels, and her books have appeared multiple times on the New York Times, USA Today, BnN, iTunes, and Amazon bestseller lists. She has received a Publisher's Weekly Starred Review for Wicked Edge, Romantic Times Reviewer Choice Nominations for Forgotten Sins and Sweet Revenge, and RT Top Picks for several of her novels. Amazon labeled Mercury Striking as one of the best romances of 2016 and Deadly Silence as one of the best romances in October. The Washington Post called Deadly Silence, "sexy and emotional." She believes strongly in luck, karma, and working her butt off…and she thinks one of the best things about being an author, unlike the lawyer she used to be, is that she can let the crazy out. Find Rebecca at: www.rebeccazanetti.com

Discover More Rebecca Zanetti

TEASED
A Dark Protectors—Reece Family Novella
By Rebecca Zanetti

The Hunter

For almost a century, the Realm's most deadly assassin, Chalton Reese, has left war and death in the past, turning instead to strategy, reason, and technology. His fingers, still stained with blood, now protect with a keyboard instead of a weapon. Until the vampire king sends him on one more mission; to hunt down a human female with the knowledge to destroy the Realm. A woman with eyes like emeralds, a brain to match his own, and a passion that might destroy them both—if the enemy on their heels doesn't do so first.

The Hunted

Olivia Roberts has foregone relationships with wimpy metro-sexuals in favor of pursuing a good story, bound and determined to uncover the truth, any truth. When her instincts start humming about missing proprietary information, she has no idea her search for a story will lead her to a ripped, sexy, and dangerous male beyond any human man. Setting aside the unbelievable fact that he's a vampire and she's his prey, she discovers that trusting him is the only chance they have to survive the danger stalking them both.

* * * *

TRICKED
A Dark Protectors—Reese Family Novella
By Rebecca Zanetti

He Might Save Her

Former police psychologist Ronni Alexander had it all before a poison attacked her heart and gave her a death sentence. Now, on her last leg, she has an opportunity to live if she mates a vampire. A real vampire. One night of sex and a good bite, and she'd live forever with no more weaknesses. Well, except for the vampire whose dominance is over the top, and who has no clue how to deal with a modern woman who can take care of herself.

She Might Kill Him

Jared Reese, who has no intention of ever mating for anything other than convenience, agrees to help out his new sister in law by saving her friend's life with a quick tussle in bed. The plan seems so simple. They'd mate, and he move on with his life and take risks as a modern pirate should. Except after one night with Ronni, one moment of her sighing his name, and he wants more than a mating of convenience. Now all he has to do is convince Ronni she wants the same thing. Good thing he's up for a good battle.

Deadly Silence
Blood Brothers Book 1
Now Available

Have you had a chance to read the Blood Brothers series? Here's an excerpt from Deadly Silence, the first book in the series. Enjoy!

The first book in a breathtaking new romantic suspense series that will appeal to fans of *New York Times* bestsellers Maya Banks, Lisa Gardner, and Lisa Jackson.

DON'T LOOK BACK

Under siege. That's how Ryker Jones feels. The Lost Bastards Investigative Agency he opened up with his blood brothers has lost a client in a brutal way. The past he can't outrun is resurfacing, threatening to drag him down in the undertow. And the beautiful woman he's been trying to keep at arm's length is in danger...and he'll destroy anything *and* anyone to keep her safe.

Paralegal Zara Remington is in over her head. She's making risky moves at work by day and indulging in an affair with a darkly dangerous PI by night. There's a lot Ryker isn't telling her and the more she uncovers, the less she wants to know. But when all hell breaks loose, Ryker may be the only one to save her. If his past doesn't catch up to them first...

Full of twists and turns you won't see coming, DEADLY SILENCE is *New York Times* bestselling author Rebecca Zanetti at her suspenseful best.

* * * *

Zara Remington brushed a stray tendril of her thick hair back from her face before checking on the lasagna. The cheese bubbled up through the noodles, while the scent of the garlic bread in the oven warmer filled the country-style kitchen. Perfect. She shut the oven door and glanced at the clock. Five minutes.

He'd be there in *five minutes.*

It had been weeks since she'd seen him, and her body was ready and primed for a tussle. *Just a tussle.* Shaking herself, she repeated the mantra she'd coined since meeting him two months ago. Temporary. They were temporary and just for fun. This was her reward for working so hard…a walk on the wild side. Even if she was the type to settle down and devote herself to one man, it wouldn't be this one.

Ryker Jones kept one foot out the door, even while naked in her bed doing things to her that were illegal in the southern states. Good damn thing she lived in Cisco. Wyoming didn't care what folks did behind closed doors. Thank God.

She hummed and eyed the red high heels waiting by the entry to the living room. They probably wouldn't last on her feet for long, but she'd greet him wearing them. While she still wore the black pencil skirt and gray silk shirt she'd donned for work, upon reading his text that he was back in town, she'd rushed to change into a scarlet bra and G-string set that matched the shoes before putting her clothes back into place.

If she was living out a fantasy, he should get one, too. The guy didn't have to know she'd worn granny-style spanx panties and a thin cotton bra all day.

A roar of motorcycle pipes echoed down her quiet street. Tingles exploded in her abdomen. Hurrying for the shoes, she bit back a wince upon slipping her feet in. The little kitten heels she'd really worn had been much more comfortable.

A minute passed and the pipes silenced.

She drew air in through her nose, counted to five, and exhaled. Calm down. Geez. She really needed to relax. The sharp rap on her front door sent her system into overdrive again.

Straightening her shoulders, she tried to balance in the heels past her comfortable sofa set, clicking on the polished hard-wood floors. She had to wipe her hands down her skirt before twisting the nob and opening the door. "Ryker," she breathed.

He didn't smile. Instead, his bluish-green eyes darkened as his gaze raked her head to toe…and back up. "I've missed you." The low rumble of his voice, just as dangerous as the motorcycle pipes, licked right where his gaze had been.

She nodded, her throat closing. He was every vision of a badass bad boy that she'd ever dreamed about. His thick black hair curled over the collar of a battered leather jacket that covered a broad and well-muscled chest. Long legs, encased in faded jeans, led to motorcycle boots. His face had been shaped with long lines and powerful strokes, and a shadow lined his cut jaw. But those eyes. Greenish-gold and fierce, they changed shades with his mood.

As she watched, those odd eyes narrowed. "What the fuck?"

She self-consciously fingered the slash of a bruise across her right cheekbone. Cover-up had concealed it well enough all day, but leave it to Ryker to notice. He didn't miss anything. God, that intrigued her. His vision was oddly sharp, and once he'd mentioned hearing an argument several doors down. She hadn't heard a thing. "It's nothing." She stepped back to allow him entrance. "I have a lasagna cooking."

He moved into her, heat and his scent of forest and leather brushing across her skin. One knuckle gently ran across the bruise. "Who hit you?" The tone held an edge of something dark.

She shut the door and moved away from his touch. "What? Who says somebody hit me?" Turning on the heel and barely keeping from landing on her butt, she walked toward the kitchen, remembering to sway her hips before making it past the couch. "I have to get dinner out or it'll burn." She kept several frozen dishes ready to go, not knowing when he'd be back in town. The domestication worked well for them both, and she liked cooking for him. Enjoyed taking care of him like that…for this brief affair, or whatever it was. "I hope you haven't eaten."

"You know I haven't." He stopped inside the kitchen. "Zara."

She gave an involuntary shiver from his low tone and drew the lasagna from the oven and bread from the warmer before turning around to see him lounging against the door jam. "Isn't this when you pour wine?" Her heart fluttered at seeing the contrast between her pretty butter-yellow cabinets and the deadly rebel calmly watching her. "I have the beer you like."

"You always have the beer I like." He didn't move a muscle, and this time, a warning thread through his words in a tone like gravel crumbling in a crusher. "I asked you a question."

She forced a smile and carried the dishes to the breakfast nook, which she'd already set with her favorite Apple patterned dinnerware and bright aqua linens. "And I asked you one." Trying to ignore the tension vibrating from him, she grasped a lighter for the candles.

A hand on her arm spun her around. She hadn't heard him move. How did he do that?

He leaned in. "Then I'll answer yours. I know what a woman looks like who's been hit. I know by the color and slant of that bruise how much force was used, how tall the guy was, and which hand he used. What I don't know…is the name of the fucker. Yet."

"How do you know all of that?" she whispered.

He lifted his head, withdrawing. "I just do."

There it was. He'd share his body and nothing else with her. She didn't even know where he lived when he wasn't on a case. From day one he'd been clear that this wasn't forever, that he wasn't interested in a future. Neither was she. He was her walk on the wild side, her first purely physical affair, and that's why he could mind his own business.

On behalf of 1001 Dark Nights,

Liz Berry and M.J. Rose would like to thank ~

Steve Berry
Doug Scofield
Kim Guidroz
Jillian Stein
InkSlinger PR
Dan Slater
Asha Hossain
Chris Graham
Pamela Jamison
Fedora Chen
Kasi Alexander
Jessica Johns
Dylan Stockton
Richard Blake
BookTrib After Dark
and Simon Lipskar

Made in the USA
Columbia, SC
15 October 2017